Dear Readers,

I've been fortunate enough to work with Cynthia Voigt on a number of books now, and my admiration for her has grown with each new manuscript that arrived in my inbox.

Teddy & Co. is a departure from the complex mystery world of Mister Max, and yet it is also quintessential Voigt, with its impeccable prose and an outstanding cast of eccentric characters.

In some ways, *Teddy & Co.* is Voigt's simplest story. It's about a group of toys—friends and neighbors whose community gets shaken up when newcomers arrive—and I know it will make a wonderful read-aloud for families with kids of all ages. There are several story arcs within the larger narrative, making it possible to read a complete adventure in an afternoon or evening.

But even a simple story from Cynthia Voigt abounds with wit and wisdom. Sometimes I see in these toys a classroom of first graders— a dozen personalities coming together and figuring out how to get along. On other readings, I imagine them as a fledgling nation working through their first conflicts of government. Now, I'm sure Cynthia didn't write the story with *that* in mind, but isn't that the beauty of literature? That each reader can find in it some fresh insight? Some personal resonance?

Plainly put, Cynthia Voigt writes literature for children. But I suspect you'll find something to delight and inspire in these pages, too.

Enjoy!

Nancy Siscoe

Nancy Siscoe
Senior Executive Editor
Alfred A. Knopf Books for Young Readers

RANDOM HOUSE

CHILDREN'S BOOKS

A DIVISION OF PENGUIN RANDOM HOUSE LLC

TITLE:	Teddy & Co.
AUTHOR:	Cynthia Voigt
ILLUSTRATOR:	Paola Zakimi
ILLUSTRATIONS:	B&W illustrations
IMPRINT:	Alfred A. Knopf Books for Young Readers
PUBLICATION DATE:	November 1, 2016
ISBN:	978-0-553-51160-4
PRICE:	$16.99 U.S./$22.99 CAN.
GLB ISBN:	978-0-553-51161-1
GLB PRICE:	$19.99 U.S./$25.99 CAN.
EBOOK ISBN:	978-0-553-51162-8
PAGES:	192
AGES:	7–10

Please send any review or mention of this book to:
Random House Children's Books Publicity Department
1745 Broadway, Mail Drop 9-1
New York, NY 10019

rhkidspublicity@penguinrandomhouse.com

Teddy & Co.

Teddy & Co.

CYNTHIA VOIGT

Illustrations by Paola Zakimi

ALFRED A. KNOPF
NEW YORK

THIS IS A BORZOI BOOK PUBLISHED BY ALFRED A. KNOPF

All rights reserved. Published in the United States by Alfred A. Knopf, an imprint of Random House Children's Books, a division of Penguin Random House LLC, New York.

Knopf, Borzoi Books, and the colophon are registered trademarks of Penguin Random House LLC.

Visit us on the Web! randomhousekids.com

Educators and librarians, for a variety of teaching tools, visit us at RHTeachersLibrarians.com

Library of Congress Cataloging-in-Publication Data
TK

The text of this book is set in 13.5-point Bulmer.

Printed in the United States of America
November 2016
10 9 8 7 6 5 4 3 2 1

First Edition

For all nine of you —C.V.

Contents

Teddy & Co.

FPO
FINAL ART TK

1

A New Day

Night was over, it was morning, and Teddy's red wagon was pulled up close to the window. Teddy was looking outside to see if the weather was good enough.

Good enough meant: Not raining.

Not good enough meant: Raining. Because if it was raining he had to stay inside, stay dry, and not go outside to see what might have happened in the darkness of night, when he was inside, sleeping.

That morning, the weather was good enough.

The night's wind had blown itself out of the sky and dragged all the clouds after. Now a yellow sun floated just over the horizon. Teddy looked out his window at the big old beech tree and the low hill behind it, where four tall pines pointed up into the sky like spears, or candles on a birthday cake. Teddy looked out his window at the new day.

From his window, everything seemed the same today as yesterday, but what if it wasn't?

"Umpah?" he called.

FPO

Final art TK

A soft gray elephant came into the room, accompanied by the sweet smells of good things baking in the oven. "Good morning, Teddy," he said. "I've made peach muffins."

Teddy wasn't thinking about muffins. He was thinking about all the things that might happen in a night. "What if we slept outside?" he wondered.

"You wouldn't want to do that," said Umpah. "There would be no roof, no windows and doors to close against cold and rain. There would be no protection from the kind of wind that was blowing last night. Didn't you hear it?"

"I don't care about those things," Teddy answered, even though he knew Umpah had the right of it.

"Houses are warmer and safer than outside. So are burrows, and caves."

"That's why they're called shelter," Teddy said. "That's what *shelter* means. But still, things happen at night, outside, all night long."

"Things also happen all *day* long," Umpah argued. "Daytime things. We go out during the day and we stay inside at night."

"But why?" asked Teddy.

"Because that's the comfortable way," Umpah explained. "Don't bother yourself thinking about it."

"It's no bother," Teddy said.

Umpah waited another pair of minutes, in case Teddy needed something else explained to him. But Teddy just stared out the window, so Umpah went back to his baking. He had no desire to sleep outside, even if there was bright moonlight and no wind. He didn't want Teddy sleeping outside either, alone, all night long. Just for one thing, what if he was frightened and Umpah was sound asleep and didn't hear him call? Or what if it suddenly started to rain, for another? How would Teddy get inside? He couldn't make his wagon move by himself.

Umpah took a damp cloth to clean the flour from the countertop.

Teddy looked out the window and tried *not* to wonder what it might be like to sleep outside, among the mysterious shadows that moonlight casts when it falls through the wide, leafy branches of a beech tree, under a sky so filled with stars that there is almost no room for black empty spaces between them. Then he saw Sid's pointed nose sticking out from his burrow under the beech tree roots.

Some nights, Teddy knew, Sid wrapped his long, striped body around one of the branches and slept outside. But Teddy couldn't do that. He didn't have Sid's long, thin shape, good for wrapping around branches. He was a brown ball of a bear. He had a furry round brown head with bright button eyes, a short brown snout and little brown ears. He had no neck and stubby arms, a round brown belly and he had lost his legs a long time ago. He knew he would fall right off any branch and plop down onto the ground.

Sid slipped out of his burrow and slid along the path to Teddy's house. He saw Teddy, but he was heading for muffins and had no time to say Good Morning. He had no time to knock, either. He slid right in through the door and went to the kitchen. Teddy heard Umpah say "I've got peach muffins."

He heard Sid say "I especially like peach muffins," and then he thought he could hear the sound of muffins being swallowed whole, one after another, one muffin, two, three, four muffins, five.

"Good," said Sid. "Thank you, Umpah. I feel better."

"Did you feel bad?" asked Umpah. "Are you sick?"

"I was only empty and now I'm full. Can Teddy come out?"

"Yes of course," Umpah said. He pulled Teddy's wagon out into the front yard and returned to his baking.

When it was only Teddy and Sid and no Umpah, Sid moved the handle of the red wagon to where Teddy's arms could reach it, then slithered around behind to put his head against the back and get it moving. Teddy steered by pushing against the handle. He pushed with his right arm to turn left and he pushed with his left arm to turn right and Sid pushed from behind and it all worked pretty well.

They went down the dirt path to the sandy beach, to see what the nighttime tide had carried in. That day, it was only a dead pine branch and some eelgrass. Sid looked, but there was nothing to eat hidden among the long black wet grasses, so he slithered back to Teddy and Umpah's red house and had a two-muffin snack.

Alone on the beach, Teddy counted the waves as they rolled gently to shore, nibbling at the sand. The tide was going out and those waves gave him an idea to wonder about. He wondered if fewer waves came up to the shore when the tide was going out than when it was coming in. So as soon as Sid returned, he said, "When I say Go, turn around to face the beech tree and start counting to one hundred. I'll count how many waves come in during that time. Then, when the tide is coming in this afternoon, I can count again while you count again too. Ready," he said, "get set—"

"I don't know how to count to one hundred," Sid said. "Can I count to twenty? I know how to count to twenty."

Teddy thought. "Can you count to twenty two times?" he asked. "Two times, one right after the other? And no rushing."

"I *can* do that," said Sid. "I think," he said. "Will it take long? Because what if I get hungry?"

"Not very long," Teddy promised. "Are you ready? Ready, get set, go!"

Teddy began to count very quietly, noticing every little wave that came creeping shyly up toward his wagon.

When Sid cried "Twenty! Twice!" Teddy stopped counting and memorized the number he'd reached, which was twenty-six.

After that they watched seagulls taking naps on top of the water.

ART TK

"Aren't they cold?" Teddy wondered.

"What do they eat?" was Sid's question, which reminded him, "Isn't it time for lunch?"

After a good lunch of banana muffins, the two friends returned to the beach. There, they saw the ospreys who had a nest in the tallest of the four pines. The ospreys spread out their wings and flew in wide circles until they saw something move in the water far below. Then the birds dove down, falling straight as stones through the air, and sometimes they caught a fish and sometimes they didn't, but it was always interesting to watch.

"They're hunting," Teddy explained to Sid.

"Hunting food," Sid explained to Teddy.

"The tide is coming in now. Let's count again," said Teddy.

"I need to eat something first," said Sid. "To keep my strength up. Counting takes a long time."

"I'll wait here," Teddy said.

When Sid came back and they counted, Teddy got a different number. It was thirty-one, so he could say "I knew it!" and feel clever.

"Knew what?" asked Sid, who didn't care about being clever.

"The water wants to be on the beach. So it hurries up onto the sand," he explained, "but when it has to leave, it goes as slowly as it can. That's what the numbers say."

Sid thought that over and decided, "You can't eat a number."

By then it was almost day's end. The sun was sliding lower, coming close to the tips of the pines, and Teddy's shadow on the sand was stretching out long in front of him, trying to touch the water. "Time to go inside," he said sadly.

"Time to eat! Almost!" Sid agreed. Working together, they got the wagon turned around and took the path to the red house.

Before he called Umpah to pull him inside for the night, Teddy looked back at the beach, then at the red-and-orange-and-pink sky spread out behind the pines. He sighed with contentment. "Do you know what tomorrow is?" he asked.

"Breakfast!" Sid answered.

"Tomorrow's a new day. Who knows what might happen tomorrow," Teddy said.

"First breakfast, then snack, and then lunch," Sid predicted.

"Look at everything that happened today," Teddy said.

"And then supper!" Sid shouted.

2

Teddy's Idea

"You know those three apple trees?" Teddy asked. He was in the kitchen, breathing in the good smell of just-baked muffins.

"The ones at the end of the path?" Umpah asked.

"Yes," said Teddy.

"Of course I do," said Umpah. "Why?"

"Do you ever wonder?" Teddy asked.

"No," said Umpah. "You're the wonderer. You're always wondering about something."

"That's because I have a round brown brain," Teddy explained, and didn't say anything more.

Umpah, who was big and soft and gray and patient, waited for a while, but Teddy just waited back at him. Finally he gave up and asked, "Don't I ever wonder *what* about those three apple trees?"

"Wonder why we always stop at the end of the path," Teddy said.

Umpah knew the answer to that one. "Because we don't know what comes after."

"If we went farther on, we could find out what comes after. That's my idea," Teddy told him.

"I was afraid of that," said Umpah. "Why do we want to do that?"

Teddy didn't have time to begin his list of reasons because at that moment Sid slipped through the kitchen door, all of his many colors bright in the morning light. "Am I interrupting anything? Like breakfast?" he asked hopefully.

"I made muffins," Umpah said.

"What kind?"

"Blueberry."

"I do especially like blueberry muffins," Sid announced.

"I know," said Umpah.

Umpah was a baker and Sid was an eater. What Teddy liked was the smells in the kitchen when Umpah baked.

"Blue is a flavorful color," said Sid, taking one muffin and swallowing it whole, then taking another.

"My idea is to go past the three apple trees," Teddy told him.

"There's no path," said Sid. "You'll miss lunch."

"We could take a picnic," Teddy said.

"I do especially enjoy picnics," said Sid, downing a third muffin.

"Maybe Peng would like to come too," said Teddy. "And Prinny. And Zia."

Umpah said, "I didn't say I was going."

"But I can't leave the path without you," Teddy reminded him.

That was true. Teddy and Sid could move the red wagon easily enough on dirt paths and packed sand, but when the way was rough or marshy or full of bushes, only Umpah was strong enough to pull or push the wagon along. Without Umpah, Teddy couldn't go past the apple trees.

Sid warned Umpah, "If Peng comes, and Prinny, and Zia, and if there is a picnic, you'll need to make more muffins."

"I don't think I *want* to go beyond the apple trees," Umpah said.

"You could still make more muffins. You could make muffins and we could have our picnic under my beech tree," Sid suggested.

Because Sid had his burrow down among the beech roots, he considered it his own personal tree.

"But don't you wonder," Teddy asked again, "what happens after the apple trees?"

"Probably nothing to eat," Sid told him.

"But I want to find out. For sure. I want to *know*," said Teddy.

"Well," said Umpah. "Whatever happens, Sid's right. We'll need more muffins. You two had better wait outside." And he pushed Teddy's wagon out into the sunlight. Sid followed them—after he'd taken the last blueberry muffin, and swallowed it.

Outside, the grass shone green and the sky shone blue. At first, Teddy and Sid stayed still, to blink away the brightness. They breathed in the salty air and listened to the little waves wash along the edge of the sandy beach. They saw three gulls flying in circles around one another and arguing about something. Then Teddy said, "You could tell Peng about my idea."

"It's a long way to Peng's cave, and uphill," Sid said. He turned to look at the rough, rocky hillside that protected everything and everybody when bad weather came down from the north. Some thick, low bushes grew among the boulders on the hillside, and many little gulleys waited for rain to fill them. Peng's cave was partway up the steepest bit, between two boulders. That was the way Peng liked to live: in a cool, shady place where it would be too much work for anyone to bother him with a visit.

"Peng will want to know about it," Teddy said.

To visit Peng's cave that sunny morning, Sid slid around behind Zia's pink house and up the hill. He slithered around rocks and bushes, across gulleys, going up and up until he arrived at Peng's doorway. Sometimes Peng pretended not to hear visitors knocking, so Sid pushed the door open and went right in.

"Knock, knock," said Peng's voice, coming from a shadowy corner. "Did I hear anybody knocking?"

"Teddy has an idea and he wants to tell it to you," Sid said.

"If he wants to tell me something, he can come where I am," said Peng.

"No he can't," said Sid, which was true.

"Humph," said Peng, because he already knew that.

"You should come."

"If I have to," he said.

He waited for Sid to politely tell him *Of course you don't have to,* but instead Sid said, "Let's go." Sid was about ready for his picnic lunch, or at least a snack.

Sid slithered and Peng waddled and eventually they arrived at the red house, where Teddy was waiting for them in his red wagon, with his idea all ready to be told. In his most excited and persuasive voice, Teddy said, "We could go beyond the end of the path! Past the apple trees! And see what comes after!"

Peng didn't like Teddy's idea. He didn't like it one bit. He didn't like anything about it. Peng was made all of wood, so it was awkward for him to turn from one side to the other. Also, it was hard for his wooden brain to change the way it thought about something. He looked over one shoulder and then turned stiffly to look over the other, to see trouble. Trou-

FPO
FINAL ART TK

ble was always on its way and Peng was always not surprised when it arrived.

He looked at the path that led through the grass to the apple trees. He couldn't see the trees, but he knew they were there, at the end of the path. He explained it to Teddy. "If you've never been to someplace before, you don't know where it is. When you don't know where someplace is, you are lost."

"Oh no!" cried Umpah, who hadn't thought of this. "I don't want to be lost," he told Teddy.

Teddy thought about that. He said, "If we always keep the Sea to the left, getting lost can't happen."

"That's all right then," Sid told Peng.

"You don't know how far the Sea goes," Peng pointed out.

"That's why I want to go past the apple trees," Teddy said. "To find out. Don't you wonder, Peng?"

"Yes," said Peng. "I do. I wonder what you will do when those clouds start to rain on you."

"Oh no!" cried Umpah. "We shouldn't go anywhere, Teddy. We could have our picnic right here, close to shelter."

"If rain starts, we can retrace our steps," Teddy announced. He liked the sound of that. Retracing their steps sounded like something real explorers might do.

"Then that's all right too," Sid told Peng.

Peng was not persuaded. "You can go if you want to, but I don't want to and I won't."

"Umpah is baking muffins for the picnic," Sid reminded him, but Peng was on the watch for trouble, not muffins.

"You'd better take umbrellas," he warned them, and waddled woodenly back to his cool cave.

"I don't have an umbrella," Sid called after him.

"It's not going to rain," called Teddy.

Peng ignored both of them.

3

Prinny and Zia Join In

When Prinny saw Peng going back behind her pink house, heading up the hill, she trotted out to catch up with him, calling, "Good morning! It's sunny!" She trotted around in front of him to block his way and Peng stopped, because he had to. "Let's go to the beach," Prinny said.

"Not today," said Peng. Prinny was young and blue and silly.

"Tomorrow?" asked Prinny. She had white and gold flowers printed all over her, so everybody wanted to be nice to her.

"It's probably going to rain," said Peng. He took two side-ways steps so he could go around her and get on home to his cave. "See those clouds? It could rain today."

"Are you sure?" asked Prinny, also stepping sideways, to continue blocking Peng's way.

FPO
Final art TK

Peng stopped again, to tell her the sad news. "You can never be sure of anything."

"Oh," said Prinny. "Oh. That's too bad. But where are you going now?"

"Home." And Peng made a quick circle around her.

She let him get by. "All right, but where have you been?"

"At Teddy's. He has an idea." Peng was ready to get back to his cool, dark cave and be alone without anyone talking at him.

"Teddy has an idea? Will he tell it to me?"

"You'll have to ask *him* about that," said Peng. He stopped to look over his shoulder, back beyond Prinny to the beech tree and beyond that to Teddy's house. He could see Teddy and Sid there, in the yard, planning something. Peng told Prinny, "It's *his* idea, and it's not a good one." Then he went on his way.

Prinny wanted to rush right over to Teddy's, but Zia had asked her not to run off without a word. Zia liked to take care of Prinny, and worry about her, so Prinny always said a word before she ran off. She went to find Zia.

In Zia's house, inside and out, everything was rosy. There were the warm pink floors and walls and chairs and tables and rugs, the pale pink plates and glasses, even a pink broom, both the handle and the brush as pink as watermelon. The pinkest thing of all in Zia's house was Zia herself.

Zia was as round and as bright a pink as a scoop of rasp-berry sherbet. Her ears were a deep, dark fuchsia, as were also her little hands and her tiny feet. Two black eyes sparkled in her bright pink face, as if she was about to go dancing, and four fat black stitches ran in a row down her soft pink belly, where long ago someone had sewn up a tear in her shining pink skin.

Zia carried an ice cream cone to lick on, and perhaps that is why she was so round that she could barely get her fuchsia hands around to the front of her bright pink self to hold her ice cream cone close enough to lick.

"Zia!" cried Prinny, running into the house. "Zia! Zia! Listen to this!"

Zia rested her pink broom against the pink wall. She took a long lick of her ice cream cone.

"Teddy has an idea!" Prinny told her.

"Oh dear," said Zia. "Oh my dearie dear."

"Do you think he'll tell it to me?" Prinny asked. "I'm going to ask him."

"I better come with you," Zia said. "I worry about that Teddy with his ideas."

Sid and Teddy were enjoying a nice quarrel about whether you should leave before there were picnic muffins even if Peng did say it might rain.

"I'm not hungry," Teddy said.

"That doesn't count because I am," Sid argued.

Prinny arrived, and Zia came right behind her, puffing a little from the hurrying. Prinny said, "Teddy! I'm here and you can tell me your idea! Will you tell it to me? Please?"

"Of course," said Teddy. "My idea is to go past the three apple trees—"

As soon as Teddy said that, Zia started shaking her head, No and No.

Teddy ignored her. "—and find out what comes after. I'm going to stay close to the Sea so I won't get lost."

"Umpah is making muffins," said Sid. Just then, Umpah came outside to join them. "We're having a picnic, aren't we, Umpah?"

"Umpah will push me, and Sid is coming too," Teddy told Prinny.

Umpah joined Zia in the head shaking. "I didn't say I'd go."

"You didn't say you wouldn't," Teddy said.

"Oh dear, Teddy, oh dearie me," said Zia. She told him, "You have no idea what you might find. It could be wild animals, tigers and lions. Or a dangerous dry desert."

But Teddy said, "It could be a wonderful garden, with a fountain and rosebushes, and singing birds. Or there could be friendly crickets and frogs. Or something new to eat."

"What kind of something new?" asked Sid.

"Can I come with you?" Prinny asked. "Can I? Please?"

Zia had more reasons not to go. "Also, you can never tell with the Sea, what it might do, what might crawl out of it. You better not get too close to the Sea," she advised Umpah. "The Sea has tides."

"Can I go with Teddy, Zia?" asked Prinny. "To see what comes after?"

"I'm afraid not," Zia said. She explained, "There won't be anyone to look after you."

Prinny said, "I don't need anyone."

Zia said firmly, "Yes you do. You're little."

"Umpah can do it," said Prinny. "Can't you, Umpah?"

"No," said Umpah. "If I *do* go, there's Teddy to push and my basket to carry."

"Then Sid can," said Prinny.

"No I can't," said Sid. "You could easily run from me on those four fast feet of yours. You never do what I tell you."

"I will now!" Prinny said.

"I'll look after you," Teddy offered, from his cushion on the wagon.

"Oh dear, Teddy, oh dearie dear. How could you save her if she fell into the water?" asked Zia. "And how could you catch her if she ran off into the bushes and was never seen again?"

"Well," said Teddy, "I guess I couldn't." He looked at Prinny. "I'm afraid you really are too little to come with us."

"I don't want to be little any more," Prinny said, and she stamped her right front foot on the ground. "When you're little, you don't ever get to do what you want." She stamped again. "Even if all you want to do is to go on a picnic and see what comes after." She began to sniffle. "I want to be big, starting right now."

"Don't be sad, Prinny," Zia said. "Don't be angry."

"Besides," said Umpah, "*I'm* bigger than anyone else, and I don't want to go beyond the apple trees, but I think I'm going to be doing it anyway."

"Besides besides," said Teddy, who had had another idea. "If we all travel together as far as the apple trees, we can have our picnic there. Then anyone who wants to, except Umpah, can go home. So Prinny can get an entire half of what she wants."

"A picnic? All together?" asked Prinny. "Can we do that, Zia? Under the apple trees?"

"And afterward, you and I will go home," Zia agreed.

"And we'll go on," said Teddy. "To see what there is to see."

4

Explorers

When they finished their picnic, Prinny and Zia went home and Umpah packed up his basket.

"Where are we going?" asked Sid.

"North," answered Teddy.

"Yes, but north where?" Sid insisted.

Umpah set the basket down in front of Teddy and gave him the wagon's handle. The big gray elephant pushed the red wagon to the shore, where there was a narrow strip of packed mud. When they reached the water's edge, he turned so that his left shoulder was closer to the water, and so was Teddy's left ear and Sid's left eye. Then he pushed the wagon forward, leaving behind the apple trees and everything familiar.

"What are we looking for?" asked Sid.

"We'll know it when we find it," answered Teddy.

"Yes, but what is it?" Sid insisted.

Umpah pushed the wagon northward, along the land's edge.

Sid stayed close to Teddy's side. He could have gone much faster alone, but he went slowly so that they could all travel on together. "With the Sea always to our left, we can't get lost," Sid explained to Umpah.

"I know," Umpah said.

"Because we can always know how to get home," Sid explained anyway.

"We're explorers!" Teddy cried out in excitement. "Explorers exploring!"

The sun shone brightly and nobody cared about the line of flat gray clouds sneaking up into the blue sky behind them.

For a long time, nobody said a word. The only sounds were the breeze brushing through the stiff marsh grass and the little waves licking at the shore, the buzz and flutter of insects, the shrieks of gulls and the occasional thump of wagon wheels when they bounced over a stone. Umpah and Sid and Teddy walked and slithered and rode along the shore, and looked and listened and didn't talk.

Until Teddy cried, "Stop!"

Umpah stopped. He looked over Teddy's head and saw what Teddy had already noticed: They had come to the edge of a stream.

"Oh no," said Sid. "Oh well. I guess we have to turn around. Will we be home in time for snack?"

The stream flowed out from among trees and rushed to join the Sea.

"Did you know we had a stream so close to our house?" Teddy asked Umpah. "I didn't."

"It's not very close," Umpah said.

"How deep do you think it is?" Teddy asked.

"I'll find out," Umpah said, and he stepped into the flowing water. It came up to his fat gray ankles and then it rose to his

FPC
final art TK

fat gray knees. He turned around and came back. "It's too deep for your wagon," he reported.

"Oh well," said Sid. "But we did discover a stream."

"I'm not looking for a stream," Teddy said. "I was looking for something else," he said, and then he had an idea. "We can explore the stream to find a place shallow enough for us to cross."

"But . . . but, Teddy, what if we get lost in the woods with nothing to eat?" Sid asked.

Teddy explained his idea. "We'll follow the stream inland, and then, after we cross it, we'll follow it back down to the Sea, and then," he said as Sid took a breath to object again, "we'll go on. With the water on our left again, so we *can't* get lost."

Sid said, "But it could take a long time to get to a shallow enough place."

"It could," Teddy agreed.

"And we don't have anything to eat," Sid said again, as patiently as he could.

"But we do," Umpah told him. "I put extra in my picnic basket. I put in muffins for a snack."

"Oh," said Sid, "that's all right then."

"Let's go," urged Teddy.

It was slightly uphill, so Umpah had to work hard to push Teddy's wagon. Sid slid along beside them through the thick grass that edged the bank of the stream, and Teddy sat up as tall as he could to see what was coming next. "Bush on the right," he would warn, or, "Big stone dead ahead."

They didn't have to follow the stream very far before the ground grew level. The stream ran shallow there, and they could cross it together, Sid holding his head up high to keep it dry and Umpah's four round feet splashing gently as he pushed the wagon through water that wasn't much deeper than a puddle.

Then they headed back to the Sea.

After the stream, there were big rocks along the shore instead of a strip of mud. Big rocks are almost impossible to push a wagon over, even if you are as strong as an elephant. So they moved a little inland, twisting their way among the trees and bushes. Sid kept an eye out, to be sure he could always see the water off to the left.

By that time, clouds were crowding close around the sun. Every now and then, one of the three travelers looked up, wondering if it was going to rain. But no one said a word about that. Instead of talking about rain, they talked about how far and how long. "How far do you think we've gone?" Teddy asked. "How long have we been gone?"

"Not so far yet. Not so long," said Umpah, only half of his attention on the questions. He had to concentrate on the job of pushing Teddy's wagon over roots and through bushy under-growth.

"When can we have our snack?" asked Sid.

"A little later, a little farther on," answered Umpah.

After another while, they saw ahead of them a long beach that curved out into the water like a rainbow curves up into the sky. Its sand was crowded with rocks. Teddy was pleased with the discovery. "I didn't know there was a rocky beach, did you?"

"We could have our snack here," Sid suggested, but, "Too many rocks," said Umpah, and he pushed on.

When the beach was behind them and they found them-selves moving through long grass—the water as always on their left—Sid said to Teddy, "We've discovered a stream and a rocky beach. What is there left to find?"

Umpah felt funny. "Is something different?" he asked.

"What's different is that the sun is hidden behind clouds," Teddy explained. He was looking all around, not wanting to miss anything. "I just want to *see*," he told Sid.

Sid didn't think that was much of an answer. They could all see that the clouds had captured the sun. Everything *did* look a little different. "We have to keep the Sea to our left," he reminded Umpah.

The explorers went on, moving through more trees and around more bushes. Then they found themselves at another beach, one that did not have rocks scattered all over it. They stopped to look at the wide strip of sand and the gray waves rushing up against it.

"Now's a good time to eat," Sid suggested. He rested his head on the edge of Teddy's wagon, close to the basket of muffins.

Umpah agreed. "I'm hungry too. It's hard work, pushing a wagon over rough ground, without any path to follow." Settling Teddy's wagon at the edge of the sand, where it wouldn't sink in, he set the basket down in front of Sid and opened it wide. Right away Sid swallowed down one muffin, then two, and, more slowly, a third. Umpah ate one, two, and three as well.

Teddy studied the water, noticing how its color had changed, reflecting the cloudy sky, and how the wind was blowing white-topped waves along its gray surface. He wasn't hungry, but something *did* feel different now. He wondered what it was.

"We can go back," Sid suggested. "We'll have to keep the Sea on our right all the way."

"I want to discover something more," Teddy said.

"Discover what kind of something more?" asked Sid. "Maybe I could go ahead and find it for you."

"I don't think so," Teddy said. "I don't know what it will be, but it has to be something new. Something from farther on. Explorers discover new things," he explained. "We can keep going, can't we, Umpah?"

But Umpah was snoring gently and didn't answer.

Sid wanted a little nap too, so they all fell quietly asleep there on the beach, with the rush of the waves for a lullaby.

5

Lost

It was a misty rain washing their faces that woke them. Sid opened his eyes first and fastest. "Oh no!" he cried. "We'd better go back right away!" He turned around so that the Sea was on his right. "We have no more food," he reminded the others. "It's a good thing we aren't lost, because in this mist it's hard to see."

"There's still daylight," Teddy argued. "I think. Don't you think, Umpah? It's not too late yet, is it?"

But Umpah didn't know, so he couldn't say, so he didn't say.

"We've come so far," Teddy said. "Let's go on just a little bit farther."

Sid looked back in the direction where home waited, such a long way behind, and he didn't want to travel alone, even if it was to be on his way home. So he stayed beside Teddy's wagon, keeping the Sea on his left.

After they were back among the trees, it seemed darker, and later, and all three of them grew a little worried. They weren't *too* worried, however, because they had one another for company. It's always easier not to be worried when you have company.

"What's the worst that can happen?" asked Teddy, as cheerfully as he could.

Sid knew the answer to that. "We don't have supper tonight. We don't have breakfast in the morning."

"That's not so bad," said Umpah, panting from the hard work of pushing Teddy's wagon. "Also, we might have to sleep outside in the rain. But the trees will shelter us."

"I've always wanted to sleep outside," Teddy said. "So everything is fine."

"Not exactly *fine*," Umpah said. "But everything will probably be all right."

They went on a little ways, until Sid asked, "Umpah, is the water still there? Can you really see it?"

Before Umpah could reassure him, Teddy cried out, "A stream! We've found another stream!"

This stream was shallow enough for them to splash easily across it, although the stones on its bottom made pushing hard and riding bouncy. After the stream, they had to make their way among dense bushes. The misty air grew darker, and they halted under the wide branches of a tall pine tree.

"Something doesn't feel right," said Sid. "I think we might be lost. Do you feel lost, Umpah?"

"I don't know," Umpah said. "We know how to get back," he said.

"Don't you wonder what's next?" Teddy asked. "Aren't those hills?" He looked off to the right, inland. "Hills with big stones?"

Sid and Umpah looked where Teddy's arm was pointing and saw high, humped, shadowy shapes with dark lumpy shapes scattered on them.

Teddy asked, "Don't you wonder about them?"

"No," said Sid.

Umpah said, "I don't think we should go any farther."

Teddy looked at Umpah and he looked at Sid. They looked right back at him.

"All right," he said, and he wasn't happy about this. "All right, if—"

"No Ifs," said Sid. "I want to go back now, Teddy. Really. I really, really want to go home. Right now."

"If what?" asked Umpah.

"If Sid goes up the nearest hill, until he can see what comes next," Teddy said. "So I can know," he explained.

Drops of heavy rain plopped onto the ground.

"Sid can go fast," Teddy reminded them, "and we can wait right here, almost out of the rain. Because we haven't found *anything.*"

He waited, but nobody said *Yes* or *No* or even *Let me think about it.* He waited some more and rain fell more quickly, as if it were glad to finally get loose from its clouds.

At last Teddy added, "And *then* we can turn around and go back home."

So Sid slipped off, speeding away. In the dim light, they

couldn't see him slide up the hill, and his return was so swift and silent that even if the rain hadn't been drumming down, they wouldn't have heard him.

"I saw a light," Sid reported. "I saw a light, or maybe two."

"How far away?" asked Umpah. "Do they look dangerous?"

Sid hadn't thought about either of those things. "Not very far," he said, then asked, "What does dangerous look like?"

"Is that all there is ahead?" Teddy asked. "What else is there?"

Sid shook his head back and forth. "There isn't anything more."

"There has to be *some*-thing," Teddy argued.

"It's just flat, I think. It's too dark and rainy to see very far," Sid reported. Then he reminded Teddy, "You said if I went and looked, we could go back. You've found out what's farther on and it's getting darker, and not just here in the woods. It's getting late, I know it."

"We'd better turn around," Umpah agreed.

Teddy did not agree. He strongly disagreed. He was having a suspicion. He was having the first faint beginnings of an idea. He said, "Let's find those lights. It's a long way back, remember. In the rain. In the dark."

Umpah reminded him, "We don't know whose lights they are. They aren't lights we know."

Teddy thought he would keep his suspicion for a surprise, so all he said was "I think the best thing for us to do is go see." The more he thought about it, the stronger his suspicion grew, and the stronger it grew, the more excited he was about it. "Which way are the lights? This way?" He pointed ahead and to the right, inland.

If his suspicion was correct, Sid's answer would be Yes.

"Yes," said Sid.

"I don't know about this . . . ," said Umpah.

"I need something to eat," said Sid, and reminded Umpah, in case he'd forgotten, "Where there's light, there's food."

"All right. I guess," said Umpah. "We can take a look."

They set off inland, traveling around the side of the rocky hill, not going very fast. The stones made it hard work for Umpah to push the wagon, so Teddy cheered him up by telling him "Not far now" every time the elephant stumbled, or grunted with effort. "It's getting close now, Umpah," Teddy said, as if he could see the lights ahead, even though he couldn't.

"You don't know," Umpah grumbled.

"But I *think* so," Teddy said.

And in fact, it wasn't very far, although to Umpah it felt like a long, hard way and the rain fell down faster on their heads, until, "There!" cried Teddy. "Look, Umpah, look there! Lights!"

Two yellow squares shone out of the rainy gloom ahead of them, shining from two windows of a little house that—if there had been sunlight to see with—they would have seen was entirely pink, a little house with pink walls, a pink roof, and a bright pink front door.

The door opened wide, and in its light they saw Prinny, with Zia behind her, and Peng behind Zia.

"You're back!" cried Prinny. "It's raining! What did you find?"

Before Teddy could answer her and tell everyone his discovery, Peng said, "You certainly took your time."

"Come right in here. Let me get you towels," said Zia. "I made hot cocoa." She hurried off to bring soft pink towels and big pink mugs of cocoa. So Teddy had to wait a little longer. He planned to tell everybody all at the same time and all together.

Finally, "You'll never guess," he began.

Prinny guessed anyway. "You got lost?"

"Not even a little bit," Teddy told her. "It's better than that."

"What can be better than getting back safe?" asked Peng, and answered himself: "Nothing."

"What can be better than something to eat?" asked Sid.

"What is it, Teddy?" asked Umpah. "What won't we guess?"

Teddy announced, "I found out that. . . . We live on an island! We walked all the way, keeping the Sea always on our left, and we came right back to where we started. So I know we have the Sea all around us."

"Oh dear, oh dearie me," said Zia. "Surrounded by water."

"Did you hear that, Sid?" asked Prinny. "We have our very own island."

"Is everything going to change now?" asked Sid. "I hope it doesn't. What will I do if everything changes because we're an island?"

"We must have always been an island," Teddy said. "We just didn't know it."

"So everything stays just the same as always?" Umpah asked.

"Except," Teddy told him, "that now we know more. We know something we didn't know before."

"*I* knew it," Peng said. "I've known it for a long time."

"You did? Really?" Teddy had hoped that he would get to surprise everyone. "You never told me."

"I thought you already knew," said Peng.

"I didn't," Teddy said. "How did *you* find out?"

"By accident," Peng said. "I was taking a swim one day, and by accident I swam all the way around. The island's not very big. In fact, it's a small island. It's not so very far from the mainland either." He looked over his shoulder to where the mainland lay, somewhere in the rainy darkness across the water, the mainland being a place where trouble might come from.

"Teddy can't swim," Umpah reminded them.

Prinny interrupted. "Neither can I! Can I learn?"

Umpah continued. "So Teddy discovered that we live on an island by thinking, not by swimming, and not by seeing it either. That was very clever of you, Teddy," he said.

"Yes it was," Teddy agreed.

Sid looked up from his mug to point out, "I helped. I went up the hill and I saw the lights."

"That's true, you did help, and so did Umpah," Teddy said. "And I'm the one who had the idea and the one who figured things out. We were real explorers and discoverers."

"And now we've come home," said Umpah.

Sid was too busy slurping up the last of his cocoa to say anything more.

6

A Discovery on the Beach

It was a sunshiny morning, and Prinny said to Zia, "What a good day to go to the beach."

"I'm cleaning house right now." Zia was sweeping the pink floor with her pink broom. "We'll go later."

"What if I went by myself and didn't have to wait?"

"You've never been to the beach by yourself and what if you fell into the water?"

"I won't go too near the water. You know that," said Prinny.

Zia did know that.

"I promise," Prinny said.

Zia also knew that Prinny kept her promises, so she said, "Oh dearie dear. Oh well. I guess," because she also knew that sometimes Prinny liked to take care of herself and not be taken care of. "I'll be there as soon as I'm finished here. It won't be long."

Prinny trotted out the door and past Sid's tree. She didn't see Sid and he didn't see her, to ask where she was going. She would have liked to tell him, *I'm going to the beach alone.* She trotted past Umpah and Teddy's red house and stopped to listen, but she didn't hear anything. She would have liked to tell them, *I'm big enough to go to the beach alone.*

Before she stepped down onto the sand, however, she stopped. She stopped because now it felt strange and different and maybe even wrong to be alone. Maybe she would rather wait for Zia. Although it was also exciting to be all alone at the beach, with the water moving restlessly before her and the noisy gulls swooping up into the sky.

But there was nobody to explain if something new and unexpected happened. Something Prinny didn't know about yet and might not know what to do about.

But it was her first time, ever, on her own, at the beach. So she took a breath and stepped down onto the sand.

That early in the day the sand was still cool from the night before. Prinny twisted her four little feet into the cool sand, then dug them in a little deeper, and then she jumped up, jumping free.

Sand sprayed up around her legs. She danced on top of the sand, pounding it with her feet, turning in circles.

Prinny was all by herself on the beach, digging and dancing. She wished there were someone there to admire her for being big enough to go to the beach alone. She looked around, hoping to catch someone watching, from the shore, from the air, from the water.

It was the kind of bright day when there were little fires running along the tops of the waves. On no other day had they been real fires, but she had never been alone on the beach before. Prinny didn't think water could catch fire, but she wasn't positive about that, and what if it did?

She watched the bright sparks carefully, being patient. After all, she knew they were only the sunlight reflecting on the waves. She knew also that the sound she could hear wasn't the whispering of invisible strangers, but just the waves meeting the sand, rushing in, rushing along.

From behind her, she heard Teddy say something to Umpah. She couldn't hear what he said, but she could hear his voice and Umpah's rumbly response. She decided everything was all right and she could go back to being glad.

This was the most exciting morning of her life! Nobody was taking care of her! She was taking care of herself!

Prinny thought she would dig a hole and let the waves fill it with water. Then she would dig a canal down to the foamy edges of the waves. If she dodged in fast to dig and dodged back fast to stay out of the water, if she finished digging and a wave rolled in, the water would run up the canal and fill the hole, making a little pool in the sand. Then she would find some small stones to line the pool and to shine under the water, and then maybe a little fish would swim up the canal to the pool.

She looked along the beach for the right place to dig, not too close to the water but not too far back, either. It was because she was looking so carefully that she noticed something strange about the life ring. *That's odd,* she thought, staring. *That looks like something* in *the life ring.*

The life ring was a round wooden ring painted bright yellow that had always rested up against the rocks at the edge of the beach. It was a yellow circle with an empty space in the center. But that morning, the space wasn't empty. There was definitely something in it. The something was lumpy and brown, mostly, but it had four somethings more sticking out of it. Were they arms and legs? Were they broken branches?

Prinny took little steps toward the thing, just a few small steps to start with, and then just a few more. She looked back and forth and all around her, at the blue water and the brightly colored houses, at Peng's stony hill and Sid's beech tree and even the distant row of four pointy-tipped pines. She watched a gull fly squawking off toward a puffy white cloud. While she looked everywhere else, her feet moved in little steps, bringing her closer to the thing in the life preserver. What was it?

Something dirty, with arms and legs, maybe four arms, or maybe four legs, or maybe two of each. She could see that now.

It had long ears too, and she thought she could see a small mouth right under its tiny nose. So it had two arms and two legs, two long ears, and a face. Also, there was something brown and dirty tied around its neck, like a wide brown collar, with ruffles.

Prinny studied the face. The eyes were shut. She leaned over close to one of the ears. "Hello?" she said. "Are you asleep?"

The eyes opened and looked at her. Then they closed again.

"Wake up!" Prinny cried.

The eyes opened. They were bright black eyes.

"Are you lost?" she asked.

"I'm quite comfortable here, thank you very much," it said, and did not move.

"You're awfully dirty," Prinny told it. "How can you be comfortable when you're so dirty?"

It didn't answer.

"Who are you?" asked Prinny, but it didn't answer that question either. She wondered if she should call to Teddy, or run and get Zia. But this was her very own discovery.

"Wake up!" she called.

The eyes opened.

"What's your name?"

"Mr. B," he said, and closed his eyes.

"Because you're a bunny," Prinny guessed. "Bunnies have long ears, I know that," she explained. "I know what bunnies look like. Bunnies are furry, and pigs aren't."

"If you say so," Mr. B answered, this time without opening his eyes. He knew he looked floppy and silly and cuddly, with the stupid ruffled collar around his neck, and a face that belonged on someone who never had a mean thought, and those long, useless ears drooping down beside his head. Inside, however, Mr. B knew he wasn't like that at all. Inside, he was sleek and selfish and sharp silver, like a knife, with sharp pointy ears that never missed a thing and secret sharp teeth. Inside, he wasn't at all what his outside looked like. He waited for the little pig to go away.

"Zia will know what to do," Prinny told him.

Mr. B said nothing. Sometimes, nothing was exactly the right thing to say, and after you said *that*, you could get back to your nap in the sun.

Prinny waited a little longer; then she trotted off.

7

Mr. B

On her way to find Zia, Prinny met up with Sid and told him about the bunny in the life ring. While she continued on to the pink house, Sid slid off to tell the news to Peng. When Teddy and Umpah heard Prinny and Zia and Sid and Peng talking excitedly on their way back to the beach, they came out of their house to find out what was going on. Nobody wanted to miss the excitement, if there was excitement. Everybody wanted to help, if help was needed.

Thus it was that the next time Mr. B felt shadows blocking the warm sunlight, he opened his eyes to see that he was surrounded. They stared down at him—the little flowery blue pig from earlier, plus another bigger, fatter, pinker one with thick black stitches down her stomach and holding, of all things, an ice cream cone out in front of her; a legless bear in a red wagon and next to him a big, long-nosed gray elephant with a thickly curled soft coat for his skin; a brightly striped snake that slithered up much too close to the life ring; and a black-and-white penguin with a bored expression in his tiny orange eyes. Mr. B noticed that, unlike all the curious others, the penguin stared off across the water, as if he wasn't a bit interested in Mr. B, as if Mr. B was just the first of many things that would be floating in on the tide that day and nothing special, nothing special at all.

Why wasn't that penguin curious about him?

Mr. B sat up. Carefully, he dusted some of the dirt off his arms and chest. Then he looked at both pigs, one after the other, then at the bear, the elephant, the snake, and finally, the penguin.

The penguin didn't notice.

Mr. B leaned back against the life ring, which had been

warmed by the sun. He was about to close his eyes for a nice nap when the little pig spoke.

"I told you," she said. "Do you think he's sick? He keeps going to sleep. His name is Mr. B. He told me."

The pink pig came up so close that her ice cream almost touched his shoulder. "Hello, Mr. B," she said.

Mr. B stared at her. It was not a friendly stare.

"Oh dear," she said. "Oh dearie me, Mr. B, are you sick?"

"Not in the least," said Mr. B.

"That's one good thing," said the pink pig. "I'm Zia, how do you do?" Then she introduced everybody, but Mr. B didn't bother listening. If he wanted to know someone's name, he could find it out for himself. After the names, she said, "You're awfully dirty and you must be uncomfortable, lying here on the grainy sand in that hard life ring. Wouldn't you like to come to my house and get cleaned up? And then, I was wondering, are you hungry?"

Mr. B considered that. "I could eat," he said. He stood up, stretched, and waited to be shown where this house was.

"Where did you come from?" asked the bear. "What's it like where you came from? Was it a city? Was it a farm? Why did you come here? This is an island."

Mr. B paid no attention to the bear.

"I could eat too," the snake said, and Mr. B paid no attention to him, either. He was waiting for the bright pink pig to lead the way.

Finally, "Maybe Mr. B is too hungry to talk," she said, and she started off.

They followed her along the dirt path that led away from the beach. Zia, shiny pink and licking steadily at her ice cream cone, was the first in line, and Mr. B was the second. He didn't look behind him to see how the others arranged themselves.

They passed a small red house that stood with its door wide open. They went by an old beech tree with its limbs and leafy branches spread wide. After the beech tree, the path led to a pink house. Zia went right in, but Mr. B stopped in the pink doorway. He turned around to stare at everybody until, without a word being spoken, they all understood that they were to come no farther. Then Mr. B nodded at them and followed Zia inside.

It wasn't long before Zia came out again, pulling the pink door closed behind her.

After that, it was a longish time, especially for Sid, who had thought he was going to eat right away. Eventually the door opened again and there stood Mr. B—a small, faded white bunny rabbit with long, floppy ears and a faded light blue ruffled corduroy collar tied around his neck.

"Don't you look nice and clean," said Umpah.

Mr. B said nothing.

Prinny came to stand in front of him. "Do you remember me?"

"You're the one who woke me up."

"I'm Prinny."

"I'll make us something to eat now," said Zia.

At that, Mr. B turned around to go back inside again. He left the door open, so after a minute's hesitation they followed and discovered that he had pulled Zia's pink rocking chair up close to the window, where the sun shone in on him. They stood a little distance away, talking quietly, in case he wanted to nap.

They were talking about where he would sleep and live. Mr. B sat in warm sunlight and listened to this conversation.

"He can stay with me," said Sid. "In my burrow. Bunnies like burrows. And besides, nobody lives with me. Prinny has Zia and Teddy has Umpah, but I don't have anybody."

"Nobody lives with me, either," said Peng. "And that's the way I like it."

"But I found him first," Prinny said.

"But I have all kinds of questions to ask him," Teddy said. "There are things I need to know. We have plenty of room."

Prinny said, "So do we," and Sid said, "So do I, a lot of room."

"Not me. I don't," said Peng.

"Mr. B will choose where he lives," Umpah decided, and this was so fair that they all had to agree with him.

Except, "He can't choose me," Peng told them.

They turned to Mr. B where he sat rocking in Zia's chair, staring at them. "You must be very tired," said Umpah.

"I could sleep," Mr. B agreed.

"Where do you want to sleep?" asked Teddy.

"And live," added Sid.

Mr. B climbed down from the rocking chair and went over to stand beside Peng.

Peng looked away, looking over his shoulder as if Mr. B were an invisible ghost, or weren't even there in the room at all. Mr. B waited right where he was, right at Peng's side. Finally, "Not possible," Peng said.

Mr. B waited some more.

"No," said Peng, still without looking at him. "Absolutely not."

"Or I could stay here," Mr. B said. He returned to Zia's rocking chair and closed his eyes.

✳   ✳   ✳

Mr. B only lived in the pink house for three days. On the morning of the fourth day he went outside—as usual—and wandered away—as usual—but he didn't come back in the afternoon for his usual nap in the sun in the rocking chair by the window.

"Oh dear, oh dearie me," said Zia, who was watching out the window and worrying. "Do you think he's lost? He was lost before we found him and he could be lost again."

Prinny went to look for the bunny. First, she went up the hill to Peng's cave. "He was here," Peng reported from the entrance, where he stood so that nobody could go inside, or see inside. "I sent him away."

"He never came here," said Sid, who was curled around his favorite low branch, from which he could see almost everything that was going on. "Do you think he might?"

At last, Prinny found Mr. B in Teddy's house, sitting on a

green pillow beside Teddy's wagon. Teddy was asking him questions. Sometimes Mr. B answered and sometimes he pretended not to hear.

"He's going to stay with us," Teddy told Prinny. "He likes Umpah's muffins."

Mr. B didn't say anything. In fact, as soon as Prinny had arrived and distracted Teddy's attention, Mr. B closed his eyes for a nap.

❊   ❊   ❊

But after a few days, Mr. B didn't return to the red house in the late afternoon. Teddy waited by his window, in case the bunny turned up, while Umpah went off to find him.

"He tried to come in here," Peng reported. "He should know better by now."

"We haven't seen him," said Zia. "Do you think he's hurt?"

Sid came to the door of his burrow. "Quiet," he whispered to Umpah. "Mr. B is here and he's asleep. He's going to stay with me. He'll see you in the morning, maybe. Did you bring us any muffins? Could you bring some in the morning?"

But Mr. B didn't stay long at Sid's, either. After a couple of days, he went back up to Peng's cave. Peng blocked the door-way and wouldn't let him in.

"I could sleep here," Mr. B suggested, the way he usually did, and he twisted and bent over, trying to look around the penguin, to see what was hidden there.

"No you couldn't," said Peng, as usual.

"But I want to," said Mr. B.

"But I don't want you to," said Peng.

"But when you don't want me to, then I want to even more," argued Mr. B.

"No," said Peng. "No and no and no." He liked living alone, waking up when he felt like it, eating just what he liked, doing exactly what he wanted all the time.

❉   ❉   ❉

So Mr. B returned to the pink house, where the two pigs wel-comed him.

"Oh, Mr. B, I was so worried about you," said Zia.

Mr. B didn't mind being worried about.

"You really live with us now!" cried Prinny.

❉   ❉   ❉

But it turned out that Mr. B wasn't going to stay in any one house, or burrow, for very long. It turned out that he liked to stay a few days here and a few days there, although never in Peng's cave, even if he always tried Peng first. And it turned out that they all got used to Mr. B moving out and moving back, staying with someone and then going off to stay with someone else. They got used to never being sure just where they might see him next, so they were always surprised, and a little alarmed, too, when Mr. B turned up on the doorstep. Which was exactly the way Mr. B liked it.

8

Teddy's Next Idea

It was a rainy afternoon. It had been a rainy morning, too. Teddy's wagon was next to the kitchen window and he was looking out at gray clouds, from which raindrops kept falling. He was busy with one of his favorite activities: thinking about things and wondering. Did the drops spill over from the edges of the clouds, he wondered, or did they ooze out through the bottom? Were they afraid to fall—into the water, onto the rocks, the grass, the leaves of the trees? Or were they trying to get away from the clouds that had been keeping them trapped inside, like he had been trapped inside, all day?

Teddy watched and wondered, and he also listened to Umpah, who put milk and eggs and butter and flour into a bowl and stirred them together. He was making muffins. The rain drummed softly outside and Umpah's big mixing spoon whooshed softly inside.

When the raindrops fell onto the sand or the ground, they soaked in and made things wet and soft. But what happened when they fell into the water, which was already wet and soft?

Teddy wondered. He knew that in the spring, when the apple blossoms blew down onto the ground, they rested there on top of the grass, but was it the same when drops of rain water landed on top of the watery sea? He watched. When rain fell on the water, the drops disappeared. Wait, Teddy said to himself then, having an idea. The raindrops *looked* like they were disappearing, but maybe they weren't. Maybe, if he had the right kind of eyes, he would see each raindrop, all of the drops that had fallen all day, all floating on the surface of the water, resting after their long fall the way apple blossoms rested on the grassy ground.

Teddy thought about resting-on, about how his house rested on the ground and his wagon rested on the floor of the house and his pillow rested on his wagon and he rested on his pillow and then he wondered—the idea blooming up in his mind all at once, the way ideas can suddenly appear, coming out of nowhere on a rainy afternoon: Why *shouldn't* Prinny learn how to swim?

"Umpah?" Teddy said, turning to look at the elephant. "We live on an island, isn't that right?"

"You know it is," he answered.

"Umpah? If you live on an island, with water all around, and if you don't know how to swim, something bad could happen, couldn't it? Maybe?"

"Of course," said Umpah. "Something bad can always happen. But I'm here to take care of you."

Teddy wasn't worried about being taken care of. He continued with his own idea. "You can swim," he said. "Peng can swim."

"Peng is a penguin and penguins swim," Umpah explained. "Like fish swim, and crabs swim. It's in their nature."

"And Sid can swim and so can Mr. B, because how else could he have gotten out to our island?"

Mr. B had been having a nice nap beside Teddy's wagon, but he woke up to speak on that subject. "Being wet is not at all pleasant."

"But you can swim, can't you?" asked Teddy.

"Of course. What do you think?"

"I think Prinny should learn how to swim," Teddy answered.

"Zia won't care for that idea," said Umpah.

"It's windy and cold and wet outside," Mr. B objected. "Nobody wants to go swimming in this weather."

"But Prinny *should* learn," said Teddy. "And we should tell her that, right away."

✢   ✢   ✢

When they arrived at the pink house, they found Sid there too. He was having a bowl of ice cream and he agreed with Teddy. "I can swim," he said. "It's easy."

"I could learn!" cried Prinny. "I want to! I want to learn how to swim!"

Zia worried. "It's dangerous in the water."

"Not if you know how to swim," Umpah said.

"But until then," Zia argued.

"When I learn it won't be dangerous!" cried Prinny, growing more and more excited by the idea, the more she imagined it. "Can I learn now?"

"Not in the rain and cold," Zia said.

"When?" asked Prinny.

"I can show you how to dive down," Sid offered, "and swoop up close and surprise everybody, and scare them."

"First, she has to float," said Umpah.

Sid said, "Peng can help. Peng can swim even faster than me, and dive deeper and stay underwater longer."

"Let's go!" cried Prinny. "I *want* to be cold and wet."

"Tomorrow," Umpah decided. "If the weather is fine, we'll go to the beach tomorrow and I'll teach Prinny how to swim."

Everybody—everybody except Zia, that is—was disappointed to have to wait for tomorrow, so Umpah invited them all back to the red house. "We'll have strawberry muffins."

"Good plan," said Sid. "I especially like strawberry muffins."

9

Prinny's Swimming Lesson

By the next morning, the clouds had left the sky, taking the rain with them. Prinny was so excited that she woke up much too early and had to wait for a very long time—or what felt to her like a very long time—for Zia to wake up too. As soon as Zia opened her eyes, Prinny asked, "Can we go now?"

But Zia said, "First, breakfast."

As soon as she said that, there was Sid looking in the window. "Have you eaten?" he asked. "I've only had a couple of muffins."

"I'm going to learn how to swim," Prinny told Sid when she opened the door and let him in. "After breakfast."

"It's easy," Sid said.

"I don't believe that," said Zia.

After breakfast, Prinny waited for what felt like another long time, until finally she said, "Can I go get Umpah now, Zia?"

Zia said, "We should wait to be sure it isn't going to rain because it's too cold to swim in the rain. We should wait to be sure there's no wind coming, because wind can make the waves high and dangerous." She was making excuses, of course.

But Prinny had waited as long as she could stand. She couldn't wait one minute longer. "I'll tell Umpah!" she cried, and trotted right on out of the pink house. "Teddy will want to watch," she said.

When they were all gathered together on the sand, even Peng, they discovered that Mr. B was already there, settled comfortably into the yellow life ring, taking a little nap in the warm sun. Although he had no interest in swimming, or in anyone learning how to swim, he didn't want to be left out when something was going on. "Do you want to sit here with me?" he asked Peng as the penguin waddled by.

"No," said Peng. He went right into the water and swam out to where it was too deep for anybody else to go.

Mr. B closed his eyes again, as if he had never opened them.

Umpah pushed the red wagon up to the edge of the water and Teddy announced to them all, "The tide is going out."

Prinny didn't care about the tide. She raced up as close as she could get to the water without having it touch her four little feet. "Umpah? I'm ready!"

"First thing, you need to get used to being wet," Umpah told Prinny. He led the little pig into the shallow water, just beyond where the waves washed up against the beach. "You splash me," he said, "and I'll shower you."

Prinny splashed as hard as she could. "I'm swimming!" she cried. "Am I swimming?"

"Not quite yet," said Umpah, and showered more water over Prinny from his long trunk.

Sid had slipped into the water. He swam in circles around Prinny and Umpah, sometimes flicking water at both of them with the end of his long tail. Mr. B stayed in the life ring and Zia stood beside him, worrying and licking at her ice cream cone. But Teddy had his wagon right up by the water's edge so he wouldn't miss anything. Every now and then, splashes of water bounced up into his face, and he laughed at the cool, salty surprise of it.

When Prinny was dripping wet, Umpah said, "Now. Now I'll stretch out my trunk and you lie down on it, on your stomach. We'll go out into deeper water and my trunk will hold you up."

"Is that a good idea?" called Zia.

"Yes!" cried Prinny, who lay down as she had been told, with Umpah's trunk under her belly to hold her up while they moved out to deeper water. "I'm swimming! Am I swimming?"

"Not quite yet," said Umpah. "Before you can swim, you have to float—just like you are now, but without my trunk holding you up."

"Don't go too far," Zia called.

"Let me go," Prinny said to Umpah, "so I can really swim."

She felt Umpah's trunk begin to slip away, and all of a sudden she felt sinky. "No! Don't let go!" But the trunk didn't come back. Prinny tried hard. She tried as hard as she could to stay on top of the water, but she kept on sinking. "Help!" she cried.

The trunk came back to hold her up.

Out of the water right beside her came a narrow snake face, smiling.

"Didn't I say it was easy?" asked Sid. "Isn't this fun?" He dove back underwater before she could answer. Swimming wasn't feeling at all easy to Prinny just then, and maybe even not much fun, but it *was* cool, and wet, and new, and exciting—as long as the trunk was there.

For a long time, Umpah walked back and forth, holding Prinny out in front of him. Prinny called back to Zia, "Look! Watch me!"

Zia watched and worried. She was so worried that she came down right to the edge of the water and didn't even notice when her fuchsia feet got wet.

"Why don't you come back in now, Prinny?" Zia called. "Isn't that enough for today?" She was so worried that she put her ice cream cone down in Teddy's wagon and forgot all about it. She was so worried that she walked so far out that her feet were completely underwater.

Teddy wasn't worrying. "What fun it must be to swim!" he cried, seeing Peng's dark head bobbing in the water and admiring Sid's bright stripes flashing along just under the surface.

Umpah held Prinny safe on his trunk and told her what to do next. "Paddle with your legs. Move them as if you were running," he explained. "When you're swimming, paddling pushes you forward."

Prinny paddled. "Like this? Zia, look! Look at me!"

"Can you paddle faster?" Umpah asked.

Prinny tried as hard as she could, concentrating on the job. Reach ahead and paddle back. Reach. Paddle. Run. Run. She tried and tried.

While Prinny paddled, Umpah carried her back and forth through the water. "Look, Zia! I'm swimming!" cried Prinny. "Am I swimming?" she asked. She thought she might be. She wanted to be.

"Not quite yet," Umpah said patiently. "Would you like me to let go of you again?"

"I don't think so," said Prinny. "Please, don't?"

Sid had grown bored with swooping around Umpah's legs and tickling at his stomach and with swimming through his legs to grab at his trunk and pull down. Umpah was so busy teaching Prinny to swim that he wasn't any fun to tease. So Sid swam away, down to the end of the beach. There, he slipped out of the water and in among the dense marsh grasses. Silent and sneaky, he slid through the grass until he was just behind

the yellow life ring. Then—without any warning, because it ruins the game to give warning—he rose up and hissed, right into Mr. B's sleeping face, "Ssss-boooo!" and Mr. B jumped. He jumped awake and he jumped up into the air and then he was gone, faster than anything, before Sid could even get one laugh out. So Sid went to sit beside Teddy.

Teddy was watching the swimming lesson, where Prinny was paddling as fast as she could and trying as hard as she could while Umpah walked back and forth, back and forth. Zia was watching the lesson too. She waded through the little waves, walking a back-and-forth path that matched theirs exactly. "Not so far!" she called. "Not so fast!"

"Look, Zia, look at me! I'm—"

Prinny was saying this when Umpah stumbled. It was only a little stumble, but it caused Umpah's head to dip down, which caused his trunk to dip down, and this caused Prinny to slip down to its very end.

"Help!" cried Prinny. There was nothing under her feet to stand on. There was only water all the way underneath her. "I can't swim! Help!"

"Oh dear, oh dearie me!" cried Zia, and she ran back to get

the yellow life ring, and then she dashed right into the water, carrying it around her neck. "I'm coming!"

While Zia was busy getting the life ring, Umpah caught the little pig in his trunk again. "I have you safe," he said.

"You let me go!" Prinny complained.

"I accidentally stumbled," Umpah said.

"I was sinking," Prinny told him.

"Do you want the lesson to be over for today?" asked Umpah.

"No, no, please? I can try harder," Prinny promised.

"I'm coming!" called Zia again, too busy going to the rescue to see that everything was now all right. She was out in deeper water by then, and it splashed up into her face. Because she had to close her eyes and shake her head to keep away the salty water, the life ring slipped off her neck and floated away. This left Zia without a life ring, in water that was deeper than her very short legs were long, and she didn't know how to swim.

"Help!" cried Zia. "I can't swim! Glug!" she said as some water rushed into the mouth she had opened to call again for help.

"What are *you* doing out here?" asked Umpah, who was busy taking care of Prinny. "You know you can't swim."

"The life ring!" called Teddy from the shore.

"Glug!" called Zia.

"Somebody get the life ring!"

"I guess if I have to," said Peng.

"Glug! Glug!"

"Zia, listen. Listen to me," said Umpah in his most un-worried voice. "Roll over onto your back and stay calm. You can float."

Zia didn't feel up to staying calm, but she tried to follow the rest of Umpah's instructions. She rolled over onto her back and—to her absolute and total surprise—she *did* float. How could that be? She was lying on her back on top of the water and looking up into the blue sky, as safe as if she were in her own bed. "Why, I'm floating," she said. "Dearie me, this is quite pleasant, isn't it?"

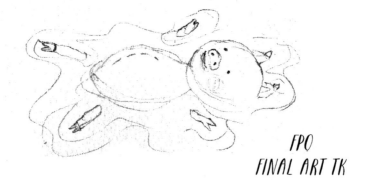

FPO
FINAL ART TK

Umpah, holding up a paddling Prinny, came closer. "You know, Zia, if you can float, you can swim," he said.

"I want to float!" cried Prinny. "Why can't *I* float too? I've been learning much longer than Zia."

"If you want to try floating, I have to let go of you."

"Don't let go!"

The bright sun hurt Zia's eyes, so she rolled over onto her stomach, where she continued floating. "Why, I *can* swim!" she said.

Passing by again, Umpah advised, "If you paddle with your legs and point your nose where you want to go, you'll swim in that direction. But don't open your mouth."

Because Umpah had proved himself such a good swimming teacher, Zia did exactly what she was told. She floated for a while, and paddled; she paddled for a while, and floated; and then she headed back to shore, where Teddy was watching from his wagon and Sid was just slipping back into the water and Peng was returning the life ring to its usual spot. Sid slipped in as Zia stood up and shook herself dry. "Swimming *is* easy," she said to him.

But Sid didn't hear her.

10

Teddy's Swimming Lesson

Sid didn't hear Zia agreeing with him because he was already swimming out as fast as he could to tell Umpah, in a low and private voice, "Teddy is sad. Maybe we should all go home and have muffins so he'll feel better."

"Oh dear," Umpah said, and without hesitating or explaining anything he splashed his way back to the beach, carrying Prinny out in front on his trunk.

Prinny didn't want to stop the lesson. "I'm not finished learning."

"You can practice by walking up and down, here where the water is shallow," Umpah told her. "Try lifting your feet off the ground. Try hard, Prinny. Concentrate. I'm sure you can do it." He was in a hurry to see what was wrong with Teddy. "Zia can help you, or Peng can."

"I've already helped," Peng objected. "I brought back the life ring. I'm not here to help," he told them.

Zia had returned to the water. She was swimming back and forth now, feeling cool and wet and safe and happy. Sid swam beside her, so Prinny was all by herself in the shallows.

When Umpah arrived at Teddy's wagon, he saw right away what Sid meant. Teddy *was* sad.

"Do you want to go home?" Umpah asked.

"Everybody can swim," said Teddy.

"Not Prinny," Umpah told him.

"Except me," said Teddy, and he sighed.

Teddy almost never sighed. Umpah couldn't think of what to say to him.

Mr. B had returned to the beach, but he wasn't stretching out for a nap in the sun. He was inside the life ring, sitting up straight, keeping an eye on Sid.

"I wish my wagon was a boat," Teddy said. "With a sail and

a rudder. If my wagon was a boat with a sail and a rudder, I could sail anywhere I wanted to go. You're small enough to fit in my wagon with me," he told Mr. B. "We could sail together and go all around the island."

"Your wagon *doesn't* have a sail," Mr. B pointed out, "and it *doesn't* have a rudder. You don't have any float to keep your wagon from sinking."

Teddy sighed. Then he sighed again and Umpah sighed with him, to keep him company, and then Teddy had another idea. Another new idea! And this was the best idea he'd had all week, even better than the idea of teaching Prinny how to swim. He said, "The lifesaver is made to float. Isn't it? I know how to steer with my handle, don't I?"

Prinny was walking by in front of him just then. She was *trying* to float on top of the water, trying as hard as she could, lifting first two feet, then three, then four off the sandy bottom. But whenever she lifted the fourth foot, one of the others shot right back down to touch bottom, and she knew she wasn't floating. "If I had the life ring, I could swim," she said, to nobody in particular.

But nobody was paying any attention to her. Prinny sighed

too, and splashed on by. Maybe, she thought, if she pretended hard enough that she was swimming, not walking, maybe everyone would believe her, and that would be almost as good as true.

Umpah had already taken the lifesaver up from around Mr. B, who sniffed and walked away to sit by himself on the sand and be cross. Nobody paid any attention to him, either.

Umpah carried the lifesaver to the water. He told Sid and Peng to hold it down, just under the surface, and keep it there while he pushed Teddy's wagon into the water and over on top of the life ring. Then Sid and Peng let go of the wooden ring and it floated up, back to the surface.

When the life ring rose up under Teddy's wagon, the wagon rode on top of the yellow ring, and it was floating on the water. Floating, the wagon rocked gently, like a boat, back and forth, up and down. Floating, it drifted away from the shore.

"Oh," said Teddy. "Oh my."

He was floating on the water all alone—although Sid and Peng and Umpah were all nearby, if he needed help. His wagon moved slowly away from the shore, and Teddy—safe on a wagon safe on a life ring—pushed with his right paw against the handle. The wagon turned left in a big slow circle. "Oh," he said. "Oh."

"Look at me!" cried Prinny. "Watch this! Watch me!" But they were all keeping close to Teddy, all except Mr. B, that is. Mr. B was off in a corner of the beach, stroking his long ears and feeling annoyed.

"This is wonderful!" called Teddy as he floated. "Isn't swimming wonderful, Prinny?"

And just then—maybe because she was looking at Teddy and being glad for him so she forgot to try as hard as she could—just then, Prinny relaxed, and suddenly she was floating too. She felt it and she knew it. For a minute, with all of her feet off the ground, she just kept on floating—floating!—and then, gently and cautiously because she didn't want to tip herself over, she tried paddling. When she paddled her legs, she moved forward through the water, staying on the surface with no trouble at all. She was swimming!

"Isn't it fun?" cried Teddy when she had paddled out to where his wagon jounced on the small waves Prinny brought with her when she swam up close.

"Yes!" cried Prinny.

ART TK

"I told you it was easy," Sid said.

"Once I learned how, it was," Prinny told him. "Before that, it was hard."

"I can swim too!" cried Zia, and she was wondering something now. She was wondering: If she floated on her back holding an ice cream cone, could she have her ice cream and swim at the same time?

11

Clara

One day Sid unwound himself from his branch of the big beech tree at just the same time that Zia opened her pink door to sweep out yesterday's dirt. So they both saw it.

Sid hung down half unwound, just staring, and Zia stood motionless, surprised and amazed, clutching her broom.

What they saw was a very large doll seated on a big white wicker chair with a high curved back and wide curved armrests, right in the grass in front of the pink house. This doll sat under a broad green umbrella from the edges of which hung a red and white and yellow fringe. The umbrella would have protected her from rain if it had been raining, or from the sun, if the sun had risen high enough in the sky to bother her.

The doll's long dress was bright white, with wide gold trim shining at its neck and wrists and hem. Her brown braids were curled around her head like a crown. She had big round brown eyes and she smiled sweetly, looking off in the direction of the apple trees, although she couldn't have seen them from where she sat. She seemed to think she was alone in the world.

Mr. B sat at her feet, leaning comfortably back against the wicker chair. He yawned.

"I'd better tell Teddy," said Sid. He finished unwinding himself and slid off along the path to the red house.

At that moment, Prinny came to find out what was keeping Zia. Prinny wasn't dumbfounded. She didn't stop in the doorway to stare and neither did she go off to find help. She trotted right up to the doll. "You're beautiful," she said.

"Yes," the doll answered pleasantly. "I am."

"And big," said Prinny.

"Yes I am," the doll agreed.

"What's your name?" asked Prinny. "Mine's Prinny."

"Clara." The doll smiled down on Prinny from her high-backed seat.

Then Umpah rushed up, going so fast that Teddy was in danger of bouncing off the wagon. "Whoop! Whee!" Teddy called. "Faster!" Then he saw Clara. "Oh," he said. "Oh my. Look, Umpah, look! Do you see her?"

Umpah, too, saw the large white chair and the big doll seated on it. He stopped in his tracks, which stopped the wagon, too, it its tracks. Umpah came to stand beside Teddy, staring just as hard.

Prinny told them, "This is Clara."

Clara inclined her head graciously at them.

"Clara, meet Teddy," said Prinny, trotting over to the red wagon. "And Umpah."

Clara inclined her head graciously at them again.

"Where's Sid?" asked Prinny.

Without taking his eyes off Clara, Teddy whispered, "He went to find Peng."

Mr. B stood up then, and stretched. He adjusted his ruff and bowed to Clara. "I am Mr. B."

After that, nobody said anything. Nobody said anything for a very long time, until all of Teddy's questions burst out of him. "Where did you come from?" he asked. "How did you get here? Did you swim? Is that real gold thread in your dress? Why are you here? Who *are* you?"

"I'm Clara," the doll said again, smiling down at them all. "I'm here to be your queen."

Peng waddled up just in time to hear this, with Sid following behind. Peng looked over his shoulder at the Sea, as if expecting to see a boat out on the water, as if hoping that Clara was about to pack up her chair and her umbrella and go away. "I don't know about that," he said, in a voice filled with warnings and doubts.

"And yes, this is real gold thread," Clara told Teddy.

"Your gold thread shines," Prinny said. She turned to Zia to point out, "We don't have a queen."

"I've never met a queen," Umpah said.

"Now you have," Clara told her graciously.

"What does a queen do?" asked Teddy.

"I rule," Clara explained. "I sit on my throne and I rule over you."

"All right, but what does that actually *mean*?" Teddy insisted, because he also had never met a queen before, or been ruled over, at least as far as he knew.

"It means you are my court and you obey me."

"I don't know about that at all," said Peng.

Clara paid no attention to him. "It means that each one of you will have a special job to do for me, a job with a title." She thought for a few seconds, then added, "It means all of you will want to make sure I'm as comfortable as I can be. For example, I need a palace, and you can build me one."

She waited while they thought about this. Sid went to be beside Teddy's wagon, to see Clara from the other side.

After a little while, Zia asked, "You mean a house of your own?"

"I mean a palace. A palace is much grander than a house, much larger and more beautiful. Until the palace has been built, my throne will be placed out here under the royal umbrella," Clara announced. "At night, I can sleep in there." She pointed toward the house Teddy shared with Umpah.

Teddy said, "We don't have a big enough bed."

"Ah," said Clara, and she waited.

"I suppose we could put pillows and cushions on the floor," Teddy suggested. "That would make a big bed."

"That will do nicely, until my palace is built," said Clara.

"What is *my* job going to be?" Prinny asked. She told Zia, "I'm going to have my own special job."

Clara hesitated before she responded to this question, and the others all waited curiously—all except Peng, that is. Peng was looking over his shoulder at the hillside and thinking about returning to his cave until this disturbance of a queen had gone away. Then Clara answered Prinny. "Your *first* job will be to introduce everyone, one by one. I will award them their titles."

"What does she mean 'titles'?" Umpah asked Teddy.

Teddy explained. "Like Sir or Lady, like Doctor or Captain or General. A title can be who you are, or it can be what you do. Not everybody has a title," he told Umpah, then corrected himself, "Except Mister and Missus and Miss and Ms. Everybody gets one of those, if they want."

"So I already have a title," said Mr. B, pleased to know that he was different from, and better than, the others.

"The titles I award are more important," said Clara. "My titles are the names of your jobs. Now, Prinny, you should do as I have asked, but first you say *Yes, Queen Clara.*"

"Yes, Queen Clara," said Prinny.

"Me first," said Sid. He slid up beside Prinny and coiled his long, many-colored body underneath himself, like a ship's rope, holding his head high. "I'm—"

Clara raised her hand to silence him. She said, "Everything must be done in the proper order, which is: First, Prinny will introduce you to me. Next, I will acknowledge you. Then, I will award you your title."

"Yes, Queen Clara," said Sid. He'd never talked to a queen before, but he liked it. When he was talking to a queen, everything he said became more important.

Prinny introduced him and Clara said, "Welcome, Sid." She told them all, "Sid will be the Royal Announcer. He will announce the rules I make so that you can obey them."

Sid liked the sound of that.

Next, Umpah pushed Teddy's wagon up to the throne and Prinny introduced him. "Welcome, Teddy," Clara said, and announced, "Teddy will be the Royal Thinker. You will have the ideas, Teddy, and you will tell me about them, and your first idea needs to be about building the royal palace."

Teddy always liked being asked to have ideas. "Yes, Queen Clara. I already have two."

"Not now," said Clara. "Not yet."

Umpah was to be the Royal Cook, to which he had no objection, since he was already a real cook. Mr. B was to be the Royal Consort, and he wasn't so sure about that so he didn't say *Yes, Queen Clara* as the others had. Instead, he asked, "What is a consort? What does a consort have to do?"

Clara told him, "A consort is a Royal Prince. He dresses elegantly—as I can see by your ruffles that you know how to do. He has graceful manners, like you. And he is always at the side of his queen. You will sleep on a pillow at my feet."

"That's all right then," said Mr. B. He liked to sleep. Mr. B bowed again. He liked bowing. It made him feel graceful and important.

Clara raised her hand to point at Peng. "Introduce him now," she said to Prinny, who obeyed. Peng didn't move forward to be introduced and he kept looking off to the side, at Teddy, but Clara pretended not to notice this lack of cooperation. "Welcome, Peng," she said.

"I don't think I need a title, do you?" Peng asked Teddy. "I know I don't want a job."

"Peng will be the Royal Advisor," Clara announced.

"I'm going home now," Peng told Teddy.

final art TK

Then Clara announced. "Since a queen always knows what to do, I will never need advice. You may leave me now, Royal Advisor," she said, speaking to Peng's back. He was already on his way up the hill.

"What about Zia?" asked Prinny. "And what about me?"

Clara looked at Zia, who still held her broom. "Welcome, Zia," she said. "I see how pink and fresh your house looks, and you look pink and fresh, too. You will be the Royal House-keeper. When I have my palace, you will keep it clean for me."

"Yes, Queen Clara," said Zia, flattered that her work had been noticed and relieved that she wasn't going to be asked to learn anything new. After all, she had just learned how to swim.

"What about me?" Prinny asked again. "What is my job, Queen Clara?" She looked up into Clara's smiling face. Really, she thought, there couldn't be anyone else so beautiful in the whole world, or with so much gold in her dress.

"You will be the Royal Princess," Clara announced.

"A real princess?" Prinny asked.

"The Royal Princess," Clara repeated.

"Teddy, did you hear? Zia? I'm a princess!"

Nobody had anything more to say. Nobody else went home. They waited quietly, feeling important. Having a queen was already very different from *not* having a queen.

12

The Reign of Queen Clara

lara let them all wait in silence for several minutes, which is what royalty and other important people do. After they had waited long enough, she bent down to speak quietly to Sid, who raised his head high to announce Queen Clara's first rule: "Every morning, first thing, everybody has to come to hear Queen Clara's orders for the day."

Then, in case anyone didn't understand, and because he liked the important way his voice sounded, he repeated the main points of the announcement. "First thing. Every morning. Everybody."

"What if Prinny is sick and needs to stay in bed?" asked Zia.

"The rule can say: Unless someone is sick," Clara agreed.

"If Prinny is sick in bed," Zia said, "I need to stay with her."

"The rule can say: Unless someone is sick and someone else needs to take care of them," Clara agreed.

"What if I have my muffins in the oven?" asked Umpah. "They'll burn and be ruined."

Clara refused this request. "You have to plan things so that doesn't happen. You'll have to wait until after the morning audience to start your muffins. Or you can get up earlier and bake them before."

She waited, in case anyone else had a request, then bent down to say something to Sid. He announced: "Now Queen Clara will give the orders for the day."

Clara stood up. "Today, Teddy will think about how to build my palace here under the beech tree, at the center of things."

Sid swiveled his head around to look at her. "But—"

Clara raised her queen's eyebrows. Nobody ever interrupts queens.

Sid interrupted anyway. "But the beech is where my burrow is. There's no room for a palace."

Clara said, "The palace will have four rooms. There will be a throne room for large assemblies, such as the morning audience. There will be a kitchen, a bedroom for me, and a special small anteroom beside the bedroom door where the Royal Consort will stay to guard my sleep."

"But—" said Mr. B, who was sitting on a red cushion at the left-hand side of the throne.

Clara leaned down to speak to Sid.

Sid announced: "Rule Two is: Nobody will speak unless the Queen has given them permission."

"Does that mean ever? All day long? No matter where we are?" Teddy wondered. He turned to ask Umpah, "Does it mean no matter who we're talking to?"

"She can't mean that," said Umpah. "That would be a very silly rule."

"Good point, Royal Thinker," said Clara. "Rule Two will begin *In the royal presence*. Announce that, Royal Announcer."

Sid announced, "In the royal presence, nobody will speak unless the Queen has given them permission."

Clara continued. "The palace will need a terrace in front, for the royal umbrella, and a garden, too, a queen's garden with roses and jasmine and a few flowering fruit trees." Then she sat back down on her throne.

They remained silent.

Eventually Clara spoke again. "When the palace is built, the Royal Housekeeper will keep it clean."

She sat quiet some more, perhaps waiting for Zia to say *But.* Zia, however, remembered Rule Two.

It was Mr. B who protested. "But," he said. She raised her eyebrows at him. He said it again: "But, Queen Clara." He had been balancing in his head his pride at being the Royal Consort against his desire to wander around wherever he liked, to live now in one house, now in another, moving on when he wanted to.

"I didn't give you permission to speak, Royal Consort," said Clara, adding, "and I don't plan to."

"Hunh," grunted Mr. B, thinking that maybe it wasn't such a great thing to be Royal Consort, reminding himself that he already had a title, which was more than anybody else had had before this queen person arrived. Moreover, she had chosen him as Royal Consort because he had a stupid ruffly ruff around his neck, which was a bad reason as far as he was concerned. Nevertheless, for the time being, he settled back down on his cushion beside the throne. Mr. B didn't do hasty things.

"Call Umpah forward," Clara said in a royal voice.

"Umpah, come forward," Sid called, although he too was having some doubts. It seemed to him that the Royal Announcer never got to mention his own thoughts.

Umpah stepped up to the throne. "Yes, Queen Clara?"

"For today's meal I want jelly doughnuts and a chocolate cake with chocolate frosting," Clara said.

"Yes, Queen Clara," Umpah said. He had made apple-spice muffins that were already cooling on a rack in the kitchen window of the red house, and so apple-spice muffins were what he would give Queen Clara to eat.

"Wait," said Clara. "I think the chocolate cake should have vanilla frosting, because the sun will be hot today and vanilla is cooler."

"Yes, Queen Clara," Umpah said again. What was the point of arguing?

"It's very hot," Prinny said. "Isn't it hot, Zia? Aren't you hot, Mr. B? I am."

Zia whispered to Prinny, "The rule. You have to ask if it's all right to talk."

"Oh," said Prinny. She thought for a little, making sure she remembered; then she asked, "May I say something, Queen Clara?"

Clara spoke to Sid.

"Prinny may speak," Sid announced.

"I'd like to go swimming," Prinny said. "It's hot and I can swim and so can everyone. We could all go swimming."

This rule Clara announced herself. "Rule Three is: There will be no going into the water."

"But—" said Prinny.

"But—" said Teddy.

"But—" said Sid and Zia and Umpah.

Mr. B moved quietly around behind the throne, snuck swiftly around behind the pink house, and then, safely out of sight, hopped into the bushes.

Clara stood up and told them, "This is Rule Four: There will be no saying *But* every time a new rule is announced." She sat

FPO
FINAL ART TK

down again on her white wicker throne with the curved back and looked over her subjects. Before anyone said anything else, she leaned over to speak to Sid.

Sid announced, "You may leave the royal presence now to go back to your jobs."

❊　❊　❊

After not very long, Queen Clara told Sid that he should call the subjects together again because it was almost time to eat and she had the eating rules to announce. Zia brought her ice cream cone with her, which made Clara cross. She spoke quietly to Sid.

"Rule Five," Sid announced. "Nobody can eat something unless it has first been offered to the Queen. And to the Royal Announcer, too?" he asked hopefully, but Clara shook her head. "And Rule Six is: Everybody will eat together."

Umpah brought out a table and chairs and set plates on the table. When they had each been given two muffins, Sid announced, "Rule Seven: Nobody can start eating until Queen Clara has taken her first bite."

As the meal went on, more rules were needed, for eating everything on your plate and for not leaving the table until the

Queen rose from her seat, for saying "Thank you for the good muffins" to Umpah and for telling Queen Clara where you were going. "How can I be a good queen if I don't know where my subjects are?" Clara explained.

When the table had been cleared, so that Zia could wash the dishes and Umpah could carry the chairs and table back into his own kitchen, Mr. B came wandering back. "Where's my muffin?" he asked.

Clara told him, "The meal is over."

Mr. B protested, "I'm hungry."

"Me too," said Sid. "There were only two muffins on my plate. That's the rule," he explained to Mr. B. "Everybody has two muffins."

"But I only want one," said Mr. B.

"Rule Four," Sid reminded him.

"But I really want the one I want," said Mr. B, who couldn't be bothered to remember rules.

A queen doesn't want any of her subjects to go hungry, so Clara called Sid over to tell him Rule Thirteen. "Rule Thirteen is: If a subject is hungry, he may request the Queen's permission to ask Umpah for a special snack," Sid announced.

If Mr. B hadn't been so very hungry and so very fond of apple-spice muffins, he would have gone off for a nap. But he was and he was and so he answered, with a bow, "May I ask Umpah for a special snack, Queen Clara?" with a bow.

When she graciously gave permission to Mr. B, Sid didn't wait one second before he asked, "And may I, too, Queen Clara?" and she had to say Yes to Sid as well. A queen has to be fair.

Then Prinny asked, "What about me?"

"You have permission to speak," Clara answered, pretending that Prinny had followed Rule Two.

"What if I'm hungry? Because I'm a she, not a he," Prinny explained. "Or Zia, because Zia always likes to be eating ice cream."

"The rule is both for hes and for shes," said Clara.

"But it says *he*," Prinny explained, not following Rule Four either.

"You'll understand when you grow up," said Clara.

"Will I still be a princess then?" asked Prinny. "Isn't a princess supposed to grow up to be a queen? When I'm Queen, what will you be?"

Clara was growing tired of these questions, so she announced, "Rule Fourteen: The Queen may sometimes ask the Royal Thinker to answer questions." Then, putting this new rule into immediate use, she said "Teddy, you explain it to Prinny."

"You *do* need a rule that says *she* as well as *he*," Teddy said.

"That's advice. You're not the Royal Advisor," Clara reminded him. "You're the Royal Thinker."

"I *think* you need another rule that says *she and he*," Teddy said.

"I told you to answer the questions the Royal Princess asked and you only answered part," Clara said. "You aren't obeying. The Royal Announcer hasn't yet returned, so I will announce Rule Fifteen myself. Rule Fifteen is: You must obey the Queen."

Teddy didn't like the sound of that, but Prinny got so excited she started jumping up and down. "When I grow up to be Queen, you'll have to obey me! That means you have to do everything I say," she explained, in case Teddy didn't understand. "It means you have to give me everything I want, right when I want it."

"Not every princess grows up to be a queen," Clara told her. "Not every queen used to be a princess. There is no rule saying a princess has to become a queen."

Prinny thought about this, just for a little. She decided, "When I am Queen, I'll make it a rule."

Teddy sighed. "There are already too many rules and this is just the first day we've had a queen."

"Rules are important," Clara said. "A queen is supposed to take care of her subjects, and how can she do that without rules?" All of a sudden, she was feeling rather stubborn about things. "Rule Sixteen," she announced sternly. "The Queen can make as many rules as she needs."

"But—" said Prinny.

Clara held up the palm of her hand to stop Prinny from saying more. "Rule Four. Rule Two," she said crossly. It was a lot of work being a queen. Clara hadn't realized how much work it might be. "You may speak," she told Prinny, but not very graciously.

"I wanted to say, I can't remember so many rules," Prinny said.

"Oh," said Clara. She sighed, and made up her mind to be kind to this young and silly subject. "That's too bad. Which ones can't you remember?"

Prinny sighed.

13

The End of the Reign
of Queen Clara

That afternoon, while Clara reigned from her throne, Teddy asked permission to ask Umpah to push his wagon down to the beach so he could think.

"Think about how to build the palace?" Clara asked.

"Maybe," Teddy said.

Umpah was wise, so he waited until they were at the waterside to ask, "Think about the rules?"

"Maybe," Teddy said. But Umpah's being so wise had cheered him up, and he told him, "To think my own thoughts."

"I'll come back in a little while," Umpah said, and he went to make gooseberry muffins.

Only Sid and Prinny remained near the throne, so Clara sent Sid to bring Zia to see her and talk about arranging the pillows for the royal bed. But Zia told Sid she was too busy just then with sweeping. Sid hadn't been ordered to come right back, so he decided it wasn't disobedience when he slid up off the hill to visit Peng. That left just Prinny with Clara.

Nobody had seen Mr. B since he had hopped away to ask Umpah for a muffin. Prinny suggested to Clara that he might be at the beach, having a nap in the life ring. She offered to go look for him, but Clara said No.

"A queen always has someone with her," she explained. "And besides, remember Rule Three."

Prinny had forgotten it.

Clara had not. "Rule Three is: No going in the water."

Prinny *had* been thinking that if she found Mr. B on the beach, she could have a quick swim—to cool off, and to feel free and floaty. She knew better than to ever go swimming alone, but if Mr. B was there, she wouldn't be alone.

Prinny was ready for a recess from being a good princess. "But I—" she began.

"No saying *But*," Clara reminded her. "Rule Four."

Prinny sighed.

A long time passed—or what felt like a long time—and nobody came before the throne, not the Royal Announcer or the Royal Thinker, not the Royal Consort, and certainly not the Royal Advisor. The Royal Cook and the Royal Housekeeper stayed busy in their own houses. Prinny and Clara sometimes caught sight of them through an open window. Once Umpah looked out the door and waved. If Zia enjoyed an ice cream cone or two—and Prinny suspected that she probably did—she enjoyed it where she couldn't be seen.

Prinny sighed.

Clara was growing cross, and there was only Prinny there to be cross at. "Rule Seventeen," she announced. "Nobody can sigh where the Queen has to hear it."

If she couldn't speak and she couldn't sigh and she couldn't leave, there was only one thing left for Prinny to do. So that's what she did. She began to cry.

The first thing Clara thought when she saw tears running down Prinny's flowery blue cheeks and heard her gulps was what Rule Eighteen was going to say. She wanted her subjects to

like her, and she knew they *should* like her, but all *they* wanted was to go away and leave her alone. She felt crosser than ever, and she started to cry too.

So there were two of them, the Princess and the Queen, weeping at one another on a sunny afternoon in the shade of the big, fringed umbrella.

After a while, Prinny sniffled into silence, and so did Clara. Prinny asked, "Why are you crying, Queen Clara?"

"Because I have to work so hard and nobody wants me to be Queen, and I don't see what *you* have to cry about."

"I want to go swimming and I want to go home. I don't want to have a queen," answered Prinny, crying again, and even more loudly this time.

Clara started weeping loudly too. "Not even me?"

"Not even you," Prinny wailed.

Of course all of this weeping and wailing brought Zia out. "Don't cry, Prinny," she said, and, "Don't cry, Queen Clara. Have a hanky." She gave them each a pink handkerchief.

Umpah had heard the sad sounds too, and he went to the beach to fetch Teddy. Teddy called Mr. B from his nap in the life ring, and being a bunny, he arrived first on the scene.

Mr. B didn't mind the weeping, but he *was* curious. "What's going on?" he asked Zia.

Zia had no idea.

"What's going on, Queen Clara?" Mr. B asked.

"*You* want me to be Queen, don't you?" she asked him, wiping at her eyes with the handkerchief. "Remember, Mr. B, if I'm not Queen, you won't be the Royal Consort."

Mr. B yawned. "Is Peng here?" he asked, as if Clara were not waiting for his answer to her question. "Shouldn't I go get him?"

Clara started to cry again.

"Oh dear, oh dearie me, Queen Clara," said Zia. "Would you like a nice ice cream cone?"

Prinny blew her nose and said, "An ice cream cone would make me feel much better. Especially a chocolate one."

"Do *you* want me for Queen?" Clara asked Zia. Before Zia could answer, Clara said, "You do, I know you do."

"Well," said Zia, who didn't want to tell the truth but also didn't like to lie. "Would you like chocolate ice cream too, Queen Clara?"

"I've been thinking," Teddy offered.

"What about you?" Clara asked him. "Do you want me for Queen?"

"I've had ideas," Teddy said. He didn't answer the question either. He knew his answer would hurt her feelings.

"You don't!" wailed Clara.

"I had *good* ideas," Teddy promised.

Nothing happened for several minutes and nothing was said. Then, as Mr. B returned, with both Peng and Sid behind him, and Zia returned, carrying two chocolate ice cream cones, Clara blew her nose in the pink hanky and took a deep, brave breath. She stood up in front of her throne and announced: "*I want me to be Queen.*" Then she sat down again. The gold trim of her dress glittered in the sun. She licked her ice cream cone and glared at them all.

They stood in front of the throne and glared back at her, except Zia, who whispered "Oh dear, oh dear" quietly to herself.

When Clara had licked away all the ice cream and chewed up the whole cone, she announced, "You *do* want me to be Queen. You just don't want to say so. It will be Rule Eighteen: Everybody has to want Clara for Queen."

"I don't think so," said Peng, and "Not me, I don't," said Mr. B.

"I'm sorry to say—" Teddy started, and Sid added quickly, "I agree with Teddy."

"Actually, I don't want *any* queen," said Umpah, and Zia said, "Oh dearie dear, this is so troubling."

"Maybe, if you were a *good* queen?" Prinny suggested hopefully.

"I'm being as good as I can be," Clara said, and started to sniffle.

Teddy thought it was time to change the subject. "My idea is about the palace."

Clara stopped sniffling. "What about my palace?"

"I was thinking maybe we could build it out by the apple trees," Teddy said. "I was thinking it would be white, like the apple blossoms in spring, with a red door, like the apples in the fall. And I was thinking," he hurried on, "maybe you could be Queen sometimes, but not all the time. And maybe there could be no rules. And Umpah could paint a gold crown right over the door of your palace," he concluded, happy at having gotten all of his ideas out without being interrupted.

Imagining this palace made Clara feel better, and she had to admit—but only to herself—that actually, it wasn't much fun being Queen, just sitting on your throne making rules. "When would I be Queen?" she asked.

"When we ask you and you say Yes, or when you ask us and we say Yes," said Teddy.

"Will we still have our same titles?" asked Sid.

"When we want to," said Teddy.

"But without rules, how will things work?" asked Clara.

Teddy thought about this. While he was thinking, Zia went to get herself an ice cream cone—a strawberry one, since now she, too, was feeling more cheerful.

"I'm leaving," said Peng, but he didn't move.

Mr. B said, "I'll go with you," but since Peng wasn't going anywhere, they both stayed where they were.

Finally Teddy said, "If we all agree about how to do something, that will be a rule."

"Like we all agree about never swimming alone?" asked Zia. "Is that a rule?"

"But what if we don't all agree?" asked Sid. "We almost never all agree," he reminded them. "That's why we needed a queen, to make rules."

Teddy thought some more. They waited some more.

"If more than half agree," he suggested.

"But what if more than half agree and I still don't?" asked Peng, who knew that most of the time he wouldn't.

"Everyone doesn't have to agree, but if more than half do, then that's the way it will be," decided Teddy. "That could be our One and Only Rule."

He looked at each one of them, one after the other, Umpah, then Zia, Sid, Peng, Mr. B, Prinny, and finally, Clara. He asked everybody, "Agreed?"

And everybody did agree, including Clara.

14

Teddy Goes to Sea

Clara was having a Queen Day and she had told Umpah she wanted a picnic lunch of strawberry pie with whipped cream and peach pie with ice cream and apple pie with cheese. However, when Umpah brought down two big baskets filled with blueberry muffins, Clara didn't complain. "You are a very fine baker, Umpah," she said.

"Thank you, Queen Clara," Umpah responded.

Clara had told Sid to announce that her throne and umbrella would be out on the beach so she could watch the swimming. She had told Prinny to tell everyone that there would be a picnic, on a green and purple plaid blanket. She had put on a bright red dress with gold trim at the neck and wrists, and a wide straw hat with a gold ribbon down the back. She told Mr. B he could rest on the blanket, since Teddy was using the life ring to keep his wagon afloat.

Except Clara and Mr. B, everybody was in the water. Teddy's wagon bobbled about wherever the waves took it, and Prinny swam beside. "Look at me!" she cried. "Watch me swim, Teddy! Look, Zia!"

Zia always looked. "Good swimming, Prinny," she called, and, "Aren't you clever?" But Teddy sometimes got tired of paying attention to Prinny. He wanted to think what it was like to swim under the water, like Peng. He wanted to watch the way Sid's bright colors slid through the water as the long snake returned to dry land.

When he got to the beach, Sid called out to Teddy, "Today is perfect!" With a snap of his neck he tossed a muffin up into the air, opening his mouth wide to catch it on the way down and swallow it whole. Ordinarily, Sid ate off a plate, but a picnic was different. "Swimming and sunshine and picnic muffins," he called. "Isn't it perfect?"

FPO
FINAL ART TK

"Almost," Teddy called back happily. "Almost."

"What do you mean *almost*?" Sid objected.

Teddy meant that something was missing, although he couldn't say exactly what and he didn't know if it was important or not. Important or not, its being missing made things only *almost* perfect.

Although, almost perfect *was* awfully good. From his wagon on top of the life ring he called back, "It's pretty wonderful!"

"I'm putting my face in, Zia!" cried Prinny. "Watch me put my face in the water!"

Umpah stood in water up to his shoulders. He filled his trunk and then sprayed cool water down over his back and tail, over his head and ears.

"Spray *me*!" cried Prinny. "Look, Teddy, Umpah is spraying me! Look, Zia!"

"Isn't Umpah clever?" said Zia. "Don't you look wet and cool, Prinny. Oh dearie me, I'm glad we learned how to swim."

Teddy floated along, watching all this, and then he watched Peng dive down under the water. Then he heard Zia squeal, "Oh!" and there was Peng's head, rising out of the water right beside her.

"What are you doing *there*?" asked Peng. "Sorry," he added, and dove back down.

"How would you like to be sprayed, Teddy?" called Umpah.

"Not one bit," Teddy said. "But thanks anyway." He didn't want water in his eyes, making it hard to see, or in his ears, making it hard to hear. He wanted to see and hear everything.

Umpah lifted his trunk up into the air and sprayed a tall fountain of water. Sunlight flashed through the drops, sometimes making small pale rainbows, sometimes making a shower of bright bits of light. Zia swam under the shower and it rained a white brightness down on her pink brightness.

Teddy watched Clara watching the swimmers, and he watched Mr. B napping at her feet with his long ears flopped back and his ruff fluffing out from under his chin. As he watched, Clara in her red dress on the white wicker throne seemed to grow smaller, and so did Mr. B, who turned into a white blob, and so did Sid, who now looked like a many-colored pile of rope and not at all like his long snake-self.

Something interesting is going on, thought Teddy as the

beach, too, grew smaller. The voices were still clear, but they seemed thinner.

What was happening?

An adventure? Maybe.

Now Teddy's day *was* perfect.

Besides, he did know what was happening: He was floating off. He was floating away.

"Look, Umpah!" cried Prinny's high voice.

"That's too far, Teddy!" he heard Clara say. Her dress was now just a bright red streak. "I order you to come back!"

"What a good swimmer you are, Prinny," said Zia, from far away

They're like voices in a remembered dream, Teddy thought. The waves pushed him gently along and swung him gently around so that now he was looking ahead, toward open Sea, and now looking back, across to a distant, dark stretch of—was that the mainland?—and now—

Now he was looking right straight across at his own island, and all he could see were trees. Even when he stretched as far around as he could get, he couldn't see the beach. But he knew that when the waves swung him in another direction, he *would* be able to see the beach, and everyone on it, so he didn't worry. Instead, he looked carefully to know what his island looked like from out on the water.

Looking so carefully, he could see things he hadn't noticed before: the bright red door of Clara's palace peeping out between the trunks of apple trees, and its white walls shining through the green of the leaves. "Come look at me," the palace seemed to be saying. "Come admire me."

Teddy wondered what his own house looked like when seen from offshore. He tried to picture the bright red walls of his house, and the open windows.

Teddy's wagon swung slowly around as he imagined things he couldn't see and saw things he hadn't imagined were there. Then he saw something new, right in front of his eyes. He saw a silver road. He saw a silver road leading away in among the trees, going into his island.

Almost immediately Teddy realized that the road was the stream he and Umpah and Sid had walked alongside of, and crossed. However, even though he now knew just what it was, it remained something mysterious and new, so Teddy stared and stared at it, to see it and remember it.

He wondered what it would be like to travel that silver road. He thought that if he looked at the bushes and stones and trees and grass of his island while he was traveling along that silver road, he would see more things he'd never noticed before. He would understand things he'd never understood before. He would have lots of new ideas.

One new idea he was already having was: That stream wasn't just an obstacle to be gotten across. It was also another path to travel.

Teddy began to think hard about how he could travel it.

Question followed question across his brain as he floated on the water, rocking gently, swaying in slow arcs. Teddy was having a very good time, seeing all these new things, thinking all these new thoughts.

He saw how each tree on his island grew out of earth, its trunk like a neck holding up its head of leafy branches to collect the sunshine, or like a leg holding up its body, with branches like arms reaching leafy fingers up to grab at the sky. He saw how the Sea stretched all the way out to the edge of the sky. He saw fluffy white clouds floating in the sky the way he was floating in the water. And he wondered what a cloud felt like when you touched it.

Teddy thought about how the trees on his island were like a tall fence. He wondered if he and everyone were all being kept inside that fence of trees. Then he saw how far the Sea stretched beyond the northern end of the island, and now he wondered if the waves rushed up against the island, trying to wash it away, in which case the fence of trees was keeping them all safe.

He wondered if floating and thinking were a new kind of exploring.

The wagon kept swinging around, and Teddy was half asleep from the rocking of the wagon and the wondering of his round brown head. It seemed to him that he had been drifting and dreaming for a very long time. He opened his eyes wide and looked around to see that he had floated past the farthest northern tip of the island and that the curved, rocky beach there was growing smaller as it drifted away behind him.

Uh-oh, thought Teddy, a little frightened now, and a little excited, too.

He wondered, *What might happen to me floating off and away like this?*

Anything could happen.

"Be brave," Teddy said to himself, speaking out loud to make sure he listened to the good advice. "Be patient."

He thought he could do both of those things, for a while at least.

"Keep your eyes open," he added, being brave and patient, and frightened and excited, all at once.

He looked across to the far-off maybe-mainland and he looked at all the water ahead. He kept his eyes open. The wagon rocked and rotated. Teddy waited patiently and bravely for whatever might happen. He tried to get ready for anything that might come next.

But he was still surprised enough to gasp "Oh!" when—

Out of the waves close beside his floating wagon, a black-and-white *thing* burst up into the air, showering water all around before it splashed back down into the water—smack!—right next to Teddy and—

Uh-oh, uh-oh, Teddy thought, closing his eyes as cool, salty water splashed up into his face. He needed to be braver than he knew how for this. He forced his eyes open to see what the thing was.

It was Peng. It was only Peng. Peng looked over one shoulder out to the open Sea, then over the other shoulder back to the island, and said, "I don't know what you were thinking of, Teddy, floating off like that."

This was just the kind of question Teddy liked. He said, "Well, at first I was thinking about—"

"Don't even start telling me," Peng interrupted. "I can't pay attention to your ideas. I'll have my hands full pushing you all the way back to the beach."

"You don't have hands," Teddy pointed out.

"Against the tide," Peng continued. "All of this exploring doesn't get you anywhere," he said.

But Teddy knew better.

15

A Rainy Day

When Teddy woke up to the sound of rain falling on the roof and the sight of rain sheeting down his window, he did not feel cheerful. "What am I going to do all day?" he asked Umpah, who was making lemon muffins.

At that moment, Sid slid in. "Are those lemon muffins? Because I especially like lemon muffins."

"I know," said Umpah, and he smiled, because cooks especially like cooking things for people who especially like to eat them.

"You especially like every muffin," grumped Teddy.

"What's wrong with you this morning?" Sid asked.

"Nothing," grumped Teddy.

"It's raining," Sid announced, as if he thought that might cure Teddy's grumps. "Raining hard," he added.

"I *know* that," Teddy grumped.

"I bet the rain goes on all day," Sid predicted cheerfully.

Teddy sighed.

Umpah decided, "After muffins, let's go over to the pink house. We can all do something together there."

"Do what?" asked Teddy.

"We'll see when we get there. There'll be something," he promised.

❉   ❉   ❉

At the pink house, Prinny and Teddy played checkers while Sid and Zia and Umpah put together a puzzle, to make a picture of children playing in a garden. It wasn't long before Clara arrived, with Mr. B at her heels.

"Where's Peng?" asked Mr. B. "I guess I better tell him where everybody is," and he went out into the rain again.

For a few quiet minutes, Clara sat and watched the game of checkers. The board was on the floor, so Prinny needed to get up and keep Teddy from falling out of the wagon when he reached down to move a checker from one square to the next. Clara hadn't watched for very long before she wanted to play too. "I could play your black pieces for you, Teddy," she offered.

"I'm doing it," Teddy said.

"But Prinny has to get up to hold you, so the game is awfully slow," Clara told him. "Also, because you stretch way over and out, you have to get all the way back up to be comfortable again." She looked at him with sly sympathy. "That must be really hard."

"We could try," Teddy said. "I guess. For this turn you should move that last black checker on the back row forward one square," Teddy said.

"You don't want to do that," said Clara. "You want to do *this*," and she moved a different black piece. "Your turn," she told Prinny.

Prinny jumped her red piece over that black piece and captured it. "Your turn," she said.

"Move the piece I said before, please," Teddy said. It was the grumpiest *please* that had ever come out of his mouth.

"Are you sure?" asked Clara. "It's not a very good move."

Mr. B came slouching back into the room. His ruffled collar was so wet he had to untie it and hang it over the back of a chair to dry. He sat down beside Prinny. "Peng doesn't want visitors, not even today."

Clara moved the black piece she wanted to move, not the one Teddy had asked her to move. "Your turn," she reminded Prinny, who was thinking about what she wanted to do next.

Mr. B reached out and moved a red piece.

"But—" said Prinny.

"Your turn," said Mr. B.

Clara jumped the black piece over his red piece and captured it. "I win!"

"No you don't," said Mr. B. "I still have pieces on the board."

"Oh," said Clara. "Move over, Teddy. You're in my way," she said. She pushed the red wagon a little bit away from the board.

"It's my turn now," said Mr. B. He reached out.

"Don't take that one!" Clara cried. "I don't want to lose it!"

"King me," said Mr. B.

FPO
FINAL ART TK

Prinny sighed, and stood up, and went to stand by Teddy. After a while, by pushing her hardest, she moved the wagon over to join Sid and Zia and Umpah, where they were working on the jigsaw puzzle on a table.

When the puzzle and games of checkers were done, Zia suggested a card game. "Go Fish," she said.

"War," said Clara.

"Oh dear, oh dearie me, Clara. War is a game for just two players and I want to play Go Fish with everyone. *And* it's my house," Zia said.

They played three games of Go Fish. Then they played three more.

After that, they had a tournament, to decide who was the checkers champion. Everybody had to play everybody else, and the player with the highest number of wins was named champion. That turned out to be Mr. B. Teddy had thought he would be the winner, so he was disappointed. Clara wanted to win everything, so she was cross. "I'm the best of everyone," Mr. B announced happily. "I'm the champion."

"Yes, you are," Umpah agreed.

"I'm getting better at games," Prinny said. "Aren't I, Zia?"

"Yes, you are. Much better," said Zia as she passed out ice cream cones, giving Sid his first.

Then it was time to go back to their own houses. Umpah pushed Teddy's wagon across the wet grass, staying under the wide branches of the beech tree for as long as he could because the leaves kept off much of the rain. Clara and Mr. B had her broad, fringed umbrella to walk under. "Good night, good night. Maybe the rain will be gone in the morning," they all said to one another. "Maybe tomorrow the sun will come out."

16

Another Rainy Day

The next day, however, was just as rainy. Teddy looked out the window at the gray and watery view. He could see drops of rain bouncing up off the surface of puddles. "Doesn't the sky ever run out of rain?" he asked.

Zia and Prinny arrived, wearing big, broad-brimmed yellow hats to keep dry. "Oh dear, Umpah," Zia said. "Oh dearie dear, what bad weather. What will we do?"

"Play checkers," suggested Prinny, adding, "Before Clara gets here."

"We did that yesterday," Teddy said.

"I'm going to make bread," Umpah decided. "Bread takes a good long time."

Sid slipped in through the door in time to hear that. "What about muffins? Everybody prefers muffins."

"I'd rather have bread," said Teddy. If it was going to keep on raining, he was going to start disagreeing about everything.

"First I'll make muffins," Umpah decided. "Then I'll make bread." He had plenty to do now, so he was happy.

"I'll sweep," Zia said, looking around. "This place could use a good sweep. But first, I'll dust," she decided. That way, she would be busy for a long time.

At that moment Clara and Mr. B splashed through the puddles and up to Teddy's door. "Good morning," said Clara, coming inside and taking off her boots. "It's still raining."

"Is Peng here yet?" asked Mr. B.

"No," Prinny told him.

"I'll go get him. It's a good thing I left my boots on."

"You'll get wet without my umbrella," Clara told him. "But it's too big for you to carry, so you'd better stay inside."

"I won't get awfully wet. I can go fast." And Mr. B was gone.

"What will we do today?" Clara asked. "I'm wearing a

yellow dress to brighten everything up. Doesn't it cheer you up to see me in my yellow dress with the gold trim?"

"I wish I had a yellow dress," Prinny said.

"You don't have *any* dresses," Teddy pointed out disagreeably.

"I wish I had any dress," said Prinny. "Zia? Why don't I have any dress?"

Umpah came out from the kitchen, taking off his apron. "Today, first thing, we will exercise," he said.

"Isn't it my job to make plans and decisions?" asked Clara.

"What do you mean, exercise?" asked the others.

"If you're cooped up inside all day, you need to exercise," Umpah said. "It keeps you from getting grouchy."

"I'm not grouchy," Teddy said disagreeably. "I'm just bored."

"Exercise is also good for boredom," Umpah told him.

Teddy did not agree. "Exercising my brain is what's good for my boredom," he said.

"You will be the leader," Umpah told him. "And the counter. You will choose the exercise, and watch to see if everybody is doing it correctly, and keep count of how many we have done."

"I want to be the leader," said Clara. "I'm the Queen."

"Not today you aren't," Teddy told her disagreeably. "We didn't vote, so you can't be." He *could* choose and count, and he could check for correctness, too. *He* wanted to be the leader. "First," he said, "toe touches."

Sid was about to say something, Teddy could see that, and he knew what it was going to be, so he didn't give Sid a chance to speak. "Toe touches or tail touches," he said. "I'll do finger touches. Everybody does what he can. Or she can," he added quickly. "Are you ready? Everybody stand up straight!"

They gathered around in front of his wagon, every one of them standing as straight as he or she could, which in Sid's case wasn't very straight at all.

FPO
FINAL ART TK

Teddy studied them. "Good," he said. "All right. Everybody ready? Then here we go. *One,* reach up. *Two,* bend down. *Three,* straighten up." He finger touched and watched and checked. Then he told them, "That's right. Now, again. One—up. Two—down. Three—up. And again, One. Two. Three." For some reason, Teddy was feeling better.

He didn't even mind when Mr. B interrupted the exercise. Mr. B came into the room, took off his boots first, and then removed his soaked ruff. He reported, "Peng wants to be left alone."

"That's the way Peng is," Zia reminded him.

"We're exercising," Teddy said.

Mr. B thought about it. He looked at the exercisers. He looked at Teddy in his red wagon. He looked at the exercisers again and finally decided that he might as well join in.

Teddy resumed business. "All right, everyone. Now. Lie down on the floor and lift your legs—or your tail—into the air," said Teddy. "We're going to do one hundred bicycle pedalings. You too, Mr. B, legs in the air. Everyone ready? And one-around, and two-around." He checked to see that the exercise was being done correctly, counting all the slow way up to one hundred. All the time he was counting, he was listing in his head every exercise he knew. He was enjoying being the leader.

After the exercising, Clara told them a story about a queen everybody liked because she was so beautiful, and she saved them from a dragon too. Then they ate fresh-baked raspberry muffins, with butter and jam. When they were finished eating, Umpah asked, "Why don't we all have a nice little nap together?" so they did that.

When they woke up, they looked out the windows and listened, and still all they could see and hear was falling rain. However, all of the leading and exercising and napping had set Teddy's brain to work and he had an idea. "We should give a play," he said.

Mr. B moved away, toward a quiet corner of the room, a corner filled up by a soft red-and-white-striped pillow, a good place for more napping.

"What play will we give?" asked Sid.

"I don't know any plays," said Prinny.

"I'll make it up," said Teddy.

"We could all make it up together," Umpah suggested.

"And then we can act it," Clara said.

"I don't know how to act," said Prinny.

"I do," Mr. B announced from his corner. He stood up and walked to the center of the room. "Watch," he told them.

Mr. B tied his ruff back around his throat and put on the wide yellow hat Prinny had worn that morning to keep off the rain. He stood up tall and looked slowly around at them all. Then he swept the hat off his head and bowed low, sweeping the hat along the floor before straightening up again, the hat now held up against his chest, as he made the announcement to Clara in a big, round voice, quite a different voice from his usual one. This new voice was excited and important and urgent.

"Your Majesty! I bring news of danger from the West. You must prepare yourself. Call out the bravest of your knights! Ladies, stay in your houses!" He pointed up at the ceiling and they all looked, to see what was wrong up there. "It's the dragon!" Mr. B cried.

"Oh dear, oh dearie me. Where is it?" asked Zia. "I can't see it!"

"It's pretend," Mr. B answered, in his ordinary voice. "It's acting."

"I could do that!" cried Prinny. "Can I try?"

All afternoon they wrote the play, and then made costumes to wear, and then acted out the scenes. First Teddy had the job of writing and then he was the director and then he was the audience, which he did especially well, calling out "Bravo! Bravo! Encore!" and "Hurray! Hurray!" He clapped as long and hard as he could.

That night, falling asleep, each one of them hoped, *Maybe tomorrow morning the rain will be gone.*

17

And Another One After That

When, for the third morning in a row, Teddy awoke to the sound of rain drumming on the roof, he closed his eyes and tried very hard to go back to sleep.

Sid had no roof and no windows, so he went to the entrance to his burrow to check the weather. Before he put his head out, he could hear rain splattering down onto the wet ground, so he turned around and went back into his dry, dark room.

From her doorway, Prinny heard how the raindrops spattered down onto the leaves of the beech tree, and all she could think to do was shut the door.

When Clara saw that it was raining, again, she felt extremely cross. The only one around to be cross at was Mr. B, so she told him, "If you think I'm going to hold my umbrella up for you when we go out today, you're wrong."

"I'm going to stay with Peng for a while," Mr. B answered. He tied his ruffled collar around his neck, even though in the rain it always got soaked through and became even more annoying than usual. If you started life out with a ruff collar around your neck, you had to wear it even if you didn't want to. He pulled on his boots and left the palace, hopping as fast as he could through the falling rain.

Clara sat by the window, looking out, feeling cross.

❊   ❊   ❊

Because she was sitting by the window, Clara saw them all coming together, to her palace. Umpah pushed Teddy's wagon while Sid slid beside it, holding a muffin pan over the round brown head to keep the bear dry. Prinny and Zia wore their wide hats, but Sid didn't mind being wet. Head high to keep the pan up, he

FPO
FINAL ART TK

slithered along through the grass, staying close to the wagon. The yellow hats, red wagon, and Sid's bright stripes gave color to the gray and rainy morning. Watching them all splash along the path, Clara was for some reason suddenly cheerful.

She opened her red door as wide as it would go. "Come in. Come in out of the rain. Take off your boots. Stay where you are while I get towels so you can dry off."

When they had dried themselves and one another, they went into the biggest room in Clara's palace, the Royal Audience Room. For a while they could only talk about the weather. "Terrible," they said, and "The ground is full of puddles," and "When will it ever end?"

"Depressing," they said, and "Boring," and "What is there to do?"

Zia told Clara, "I'll dust and sweep. I'll clean the palace. I've never cleaned a palace, and I've already cleaned my pink house three times and Teddy's red house twice. So may I do yours today? Please?"

"Of course," said Clara. Then she asked hopefully, "Shall I be Queen today?"

"Why would we want a queen for today?" asked Teddy.

"Because it's *my* palace and because I know some good pretends," Clara said. "Also, I have checkers and Parcheesi, and I have a jigsaw puzzle that's a map of the world."

"The whole world?" asked Teddy. "All of it? We could do the puzzle first," he suggested. "We could do the puzzle now."

They voted, and Clara was Queen for that day. Now both Clara and Zia were happy, and so was Umpah, who went off to make cheese muffins. "In this weather, everybody needs hearty food," he said.

Clara told the Royal Announcer to announce the first activity. Sid was pleased to be important again. He announced, "We will play Parcheesi."

"But—" Teddy began.

Queen Clara held up her hand. "Rule Four," she said. "Announce it," she told Sid, who said, "Rule Four."

Teddy sighed.

"I can't remember the rules," Prinny whispered to Zia.

"You're a princess today," Zia whispered back. "You don't have to remember."

Clara told the Royal Announcer to announce the game again, so Sid said, "We will play Parcheesi."

"I wanted to do the puzzle first," Teddy said sadly, maybe speaking to Umpah, maybe just to himself.

Clara brought out the Parcheesi set. They were all in *her* palace playing *her* game, and that was the way she liked things.

Sid had a long board game to play, a game with lots of rules and a long twisting path to follow all around the board. He got to make the announcements and play a long game and, in a little while, smell the good hearty smell of cheese muffins baking in the oven. He was happy.

When Teddy's blue pieces were on the opposite side of the board from his wagon, Prinny moved his blue ones and her red ones too. So half of the time, Prinny got to play twice as much as anyone else, which made her happy.

They had only just started when Mr. B returned. He took off his wet ruff and his boots. He sat down at the Parcheesi board. He didn't say a word about Peng and he didn't have to. Instead, "I'm green," Mr. B told them, and then he said, "I should get a turn right now, to catch up. I bet Peng will get tired of being alone all the time," he decided, and that thought cheered him up. "He might even want me to stay with him. Maybe tonight."

While they rolled the dice and moved their pieces around

the Parcheesi board, they talked about how different Peng was from everybody else. "He doesn't like us the way we like us," Prinny explained.

"He's very different from us," Clara decided.

"Aren't we all different?" asked Teddy. "Each one of us?"

That very interesting idea started to cheer him up, but when Zia said, "I wish Peng would want to spend the day with us," and the others agreed with her, Teddy sighed. Again.

"He doesn't want to," Mr. B told them.

"But he does like us," Prinny said. "In his different way. He likes living on our island with us, when we're outside especially, especially when we're swimming."

They played on, moving their pieces in a race to Home. While they played they talked about what Peng might be doing, all alone on all these long rainy days, and about how much they didn't like this weather. Then they talked about other days—"Remember when we went exploring?"—days when the sun was shining warm onto the island—"Remember when Prinny and Zia learned to swim?"

After Parcheesi, it was time to eat the very good cheese muffins Umpah had made. After the muffins, Clara told Sid to announce that it was time for the jigsaw puzzle. They set the pieces out on a table and everyone worked on it together. Teddy watched as the seven seas and the five continents took shape. He put together pieces and also suggested pieces for others to try. "Sid, maybe that white piece is the Himalayas, which are very high mountains and always covered with snow. No, not *that* white piece, the one three away from it. No, not that one, three away in the other direction, toward me. I said, the *white* piece." And he sighed, because he would have liked to do the jigsaw puzzle all by himself and he knew he wasn't supposed to have such an unfriendly idea.

It took a long time to finish the puzzle, but when it was done, Teddy could see what the whole world looked like all put together, with its mountain ranges and islands, all the different countries and the long rivers. He thought about how large the whole world was all put together, and how small a bear in a red wagon was, compared to the whole world. He guessed that a bear in a red wagon didn't matter very much, not compared to the whole world. That was an interesting idea, although not a cheerful one.

In the late afternoon Clara held a pretend tea party, with real cups and saucers, and a real china teapot for the pretend tea. She had a special silver plate to hold pretend cookies, and pretend slices of cake, and pretend thin sandwiches cut into triangles. "You have to drink and eat politely," Clara said, showing them how to sip from the teacup. "Today we are playing at *my* house," she reminded Sid, who wasn't interested in pretend food. "I'm the Queen," she reminded Mr. B, who tried to sneak away for a nap. "At tea, you talk politely," she told them.

Everybody tried to talk politely, except Teddy, who wasn't talking at all. He was wondering why a bear had to be so small when the world was so large. He was wondering why nobody else liked thinking more than eating or swimming, or pretending.

Then Sid said he hoped that if it rained the next day—which he hoped it wouldn't, and they agreed with him about that—but *if* it did, he wanted them to come to his burrow.

"You don't have games or puzzles," Mr. B said.

"I want to have a turn," Sid said.

"If there's nothing to do, what can we do all day in Sid's burrow?" Prinny asked. "Teddy? Do you have an idea?"

Teddy didn't answer. He only sighed.

"Your burrow is too small and dirty for any queen to go into," Clara said. "Everybody better come back here."

"But it's my turn to have a turn," Sid said.

"Oh dearie me, Sid," said Zia. "There's nothing for me to do in your burrow. The floor is dirt, so if I sweep I'll sweep away your floor."

"But—" Sid started.

"There's no oven," Umpah said, speaking softly. He hoped that if he said it softly, maybe Sid wouldn't mind. "You don't want to go all day without muffins, do you?"

"Of course not," said Sid, and for some reason those muffins made him feel cheery again. "What kind of muffins will they be, tomorrow?"

"Rain or shine, we'll have peach muffins," Umpah promised.

"We want *shine!*" they all cried in loud and hopeful voices— all except Teddy, that is.

18

Prinny's Good Idea

It was when everyone else was busy yelling out their sunshine hopes and Teddy didn't join in that Prinny started to wonder. Once she started to wonder, she began to remember that Teddy hadn't said anything much since the jigsaw puzzle, not about the muffins, not about the tea party, and not even to think up an excuse to not spend a day in Sid's dark, chilly burrow.

What was wrong with Teddy?

Maybe nothing. Probably nothing.

But Teddy usually talked more than anyone else and had more ideas to talk about too.

That night, when Prinny went to bed, she heard the rain drumming on her roof and the wind curling around the eaves of the pink house and she thought about Teddy. It took her longer than usual to fall asleep.

When rain woke her up the next morning, the idea that had been dancing around the edges of her dreams jumped right up in front of her face.

A party!

A party for Teddy!!

A surprise party for Teddy!!!

Not a birthday party, because it wasn't his birthday, and not a party Teddy gave, because the party was to cheer Teddy up. Because it seemed to Prinny that when Teddy didn't have any ideas or anything to say on any subject, he might be feeling sad. And it seemed to her that if Teddy was sad, she wanted to cheer him up. Prinny knew that when she needed cheering up, she liked people to pay attention to her, and do nice things for her, give her presents—

They could all give presents to Teddy!

They could have a present party for Teddy!!

A surprise present party!!!

She ran to tell Zia. "I had an idea! I had a really good idea, Zia! Why don't we give Teddy a surprise present party to cheer him up?"

Zia had doubts. "It's a kind thought, Prinny, but there has been too much rain for too many days and I don't think anyone feels like doing anything today."

"Not today, tomorrow," Prinny said. "Maybe the sun will come out tomorrow."

"I don't know about that," said Zia. "I suppose I *could* give him some ice cream. Chocolate ice cream is always a treat."

Prinny put on her yellow rain hat and splashed over to Sid's burrow. "I want to give Teddy a party," she said.

"I don't feel like doing anything today," said Sid.

"Not a party today. A party tomorrow," Prinny said. "Today you can think of a present."

"I can't think of anything, in all this rain," said Sid.

"Just try," Prinny urged him. She waited while Sid curled and uncurled himself, trying.

At last Sid said, "Teddy likes games."

"Do you have any games you can give him?" Prinny asked.

"You know I don't," Sid said. He coiled and uncoiled, thinking. "Not a single one. But—you know?" he asked her, rising up tall, almost onto the tip of his tail, in sudden excitement, "I could make one up. I could make up a game, maybe with counting, and with words, too, and I could give that to Teddy, for a present. We could all play, and there could be prizes for the winners," Sid said, and he realized, "The prizes could be muffins!"

Reminded, he opened a cupboard door and took out a plate of muffins. "I need food for thought," he said. "You'd better go away now, Prinny. I have some serious thinking to do."

Next, Prinny went to Clara's palace, where she found Clara looking out at the rain. "Good morning, Prinny," Clara said. "We're not going anywhere and we're not doing anything." She sighed.

Mr. B opened his eyes and said, "I'm trying to sleep and you are disturbing me." He closed his eyes again.

"We should have a party tomorrow, for Teddy, with presents. Don't you want to?" asked Prinny. "It's my very own idea!"

Mr. B decided to stay awake. "Will we all get presents?"

"No," Prinny told him. "We'll all *give* presents, to Teddy."

"Why?" asked Mr. B.

"Because he's sad," said Prinny.

"I have a hat," Clara said. "I have a blue straw hat I could give him, with a long green ribbon. He'd like that. A hat would make the best present."

"I suppose I could give him my ruff," said Mr. B. "Teddy would like wearing my ruff." This was the perfect present, he thought. He was getting rid of something he didn't want and giving it to someone who might like it. "I can wrap it up in tissue paper and tie a bow around it."

"What if it rains tomorrow?" asked Clara.

"Maybe it won't rain," Prinny said.

"But if it *is* still raining, we could have the party right here in the Royal Audience Room," Clara decided. "I better find some decorations," she said. "Come help me, Mr. B. We have an awful lot to do. We're too busy to play with you today, Prinny. You may leave us. Right now."

So Prinny went to tell Peng her idea.

When Peng opened his round door to Prinny, all he said was "You're not Mr. B." He didn't say *Please come in* or even *Hello*.

"I have an idea," Prinny said as rain splashed down around her.

"I thought that today I might go for a walk with Mr. B," Peng said. "If you had been him, I would have told you that. I thought that we might go to wherever it is he goes off to every day. With all this rain, I'm not getting enough exercise."

"You can walk with me instead," Prinny offered.

While they went down the hill, she told him her plan.

"Tomorrow is awfully soon," Peng pointed out. "It's not as if I have a closet full of presents."

"You can think of something."

"Maybe," he agreed. "Maybe not," he pointed out.

Peng didn't tell Prinny this, but he had already decided on his present. He would give Teddy one of the lucky stones that sometimes washed up on the island. He had a small collection of the dark gray white-belted stones that brought good luck to whoever had them. Maybe he would give Teddy two.

Peng didn't tell Prinny this, either, but he had to admit that three days was a long time to be alone on your own, all the time, with nothing to do except think up new ways to say No to Mr. B.

"I'd better go to the palace," he said to the little pig. "Mr. B will want to ask my advice. Goodbye, Prinny."

At the red house, Teddy was sitting beside the window, looking out at the bad weather, and Umpah was out in his kitchen, but neither one of them was busy.

"This rain stinks," Teddy said to Prinny. Then he turned to look out the window again. "I don't know why you came over."

Prinny went out to the kitchen.

"There are no peach muffins left, I'm afraid," said Umpah. "Sid took all of them and it's too rainy to make more."

"Oh dear," Prinny said. "That's bad news." In a soft, soft voice, she explained her idea to Umpah, ending, "I hoped you would make the muffins for your present."

"Oh," Umpah said. "Oh, well, in that case, if it's a special occasion, maybe I can. Maybe I will. Maybe I could make blueberry muffins. Or maybe I could make a cake. Or maybe? I could make a cake out of blueberry muffins. I could make a circle of blueberry muffins to be the bottom layer and I could put more circle layers on top. Each layer could be smaller than the one below. I wonder how tall I can make it. And I'll need a present, too."

"Do you have one?" Prinny asked. She had thought that the blueberry muffin cake was Umpah's present, but two presents are always better than one.

"I haven't given Teddy a present for a long time. I can't think of what— Oh!" said Umpah, and he rushed around the table. "I have to go see Zia. Will you stay with Teddy while I'm gone? Because I'll need her help with my idea for a special present, and I don't want Teddy to be lonely." He headed out the door, into the rain. "There's so much to do! I hope I have enough time."

Teddy didn't even ask Umpah where he was going. He didn't ask Prinny why she was staying. All he said was "This rain really stinks."

"Why are you such a Gloomy Gus today?" Prinny asked. She herself was feeling pretty cheerful, what with all this thinking about presents to give and parties to keep a secret.

"Gloomy Gus," said Teddy. "Gloomy Gus. That's like a sad sack."

"It's like Sad Sally," Prinny told him. "Because *Gus* is a name and *sack* isn't."

"Happy Harry," said Teddy.

"Merry Mary," said Prinny.

"Angry Andy."

"Mad Marilyn."

They went name-calling back and forth around the alphabet. Q and Y were difficult, "Maybe impossible," Teddy said, but then he remembered, "Quentin!"

Prinny added, "Quiet. Quiet Quentin," and said, "Yellow?"

"Yolanda!" cried Teddy.

They could only think of one pair of words for Z, Zany Zachariah, and for a long time it looked as if they'd need to skip X. Until Prinny asked, "Isn't Xavier a name?" and Teddy laughed. "Xtra-special Xavier!" he cried.

That night, Prinny was almost too excited to go to sleep. She was drifting off, thinking that if *Quentin* really was a name there were lots of words besides *Quiet*. There was Quarrelsome Quentin and Quick Quentin and Quivering Quentin too. She wondered how Teddy would look wearing Mr. B's ruff and Clara's blue straw hat with a long green ribbon down the back. She was busy wondering what Umpah's present idea was, when she had a terrible thought.

"Zia!" she called. "Zia, come quick!"

Zia rushed in. "Oh dear, oh dearie dear, Prinny, what is it? What's wrong?"

"Everybody has a present to give Teddy tomorrow! But I don't have any!" cried Prinny. "I don't have any present to give him! And it will probably rain!" All the cheerfulness of having her very own good idea was melting away.

Zia just laughed, but nicely. "Don't you know, Prinny? The whole party is your present," Zia said.

"It is?" asked Prinny.

"Imagine how Teddy will feel," Zia said.

Prinny did. She imagined it all, and then she decided: "It is!"

19

Teddy's Party

As she was falling asleep to the sound of falling rain, Prinny kept on imagining about Teddy's party. She imagined how the table would look, piled with brightly wrapped presents, with a blueberry muffin cake right in the middle. She imagined all the guests waiting on the beach for Teddy to arrive. She even imagined a bright sun high in a blue sky. And in fact, the next morning the sun did come out, to shine down warm and bright on Teddy's Surprise Present Party, just the way Prinny wanted.

When Umpah pushed the red wagon down to the beach, Teddy saw: a round table, four wrapped boxes in different shapes on the table, a round muffin cake three layers high in the middle of the table right next to a bowl of chocolate ice cream cones, and, tucked under the table, a strange lumpy-shaped thing, covered by a pink sheet. He also saw that everyone was there, even Peng, and he heard their shout as soon as he came into view.

"Surprise! Surprise!" they shouted.

"Surprise?" asked Teddy. "For me? Why?"

"Because," Prinny explained, and Teddy didn't really care if that wasn't a real reason.

"Are those presents for me?" he asked.

"Yes!" Prinny said. She was so excited that her four little feet kept dancing her around. "And the cake is from Umpah!"

"Oh. Thank you, Umpah," Teddy said. "It looks delicious."

"Would you like me to take a taste to test it?" Sid offered.

"No thank you," Teddy said, and he wanted to laugh.

"And the ice cream cones are from me," Zia said. "We should have them before the ice cream melts away. It's chocolate," she told Teddy.

ART TK

"Chocolate ice cream is the best kind," Teddy said. "Thank you, Zia."

"I'll start passing the bowl for you," Sid offered. "I'll take my cone now," and this time Teddy did laugh, a friendly little laugh so as not to hurt Sid's feelings.

"What's that big pink lumpy shape?" Teddy asked.

"First, open this," said Clara, and she passed him a round package in gold paper with a gold ribbon around it.

Teddy put the hat right on, and he moved his head back and forth to feel the green ribbon floating up against his back. "Thank you, Clara. It's the first hat I ever had," he said. "Do you know what's under the pink sheet?"

Of course she didn't. Then Mr. B put a lumpy soft package wrapped in blue paper into Teddy's arms. "Now mine," he insisted.

"You've lost your ruff," Teddy observed.

"No I haven't," said Mr. B. "Open it."

"Oh," Teddy said, when he saw what Mr. B had given him. "Are you sure you want me to have this?"

Mr. B was positive. "I'll tie it for you," he offered.

But Teddy's neck was too fat for the ruff to go around. For a minute, Mr. B was afraid he'd have to take it back and think of another present, but then Teddy said, "It would be perfect for a bracelet. Can you tie it around my wrist?" and that problem was solved. When Teddy sat so splendidly attired in his wagon, with the blue straw hat on his head and the green ribbon down his back and the ruffled bracelet around his wrist, everybody said he looked like a bear dressed up for a Surprise Present Party.

"That's what I look like because that's what I am!" cried Teddy. "Thank you for the bracelet, Mr. B," he said happily.

"You are very welcome," said Mr. B, just as happily. He'd known it was the perfect gift.

"What about that strange, big—" Teddy began, but Peng had gone up close to the table, and looked away from a little package wrapped in plain white paper with a plain black bow, as if he didn't care about it one little bit.

Of course Teddy understood. The more Peng wanted everyone to think he didn't care, the more he really cared. So, "Will someone please pass me that little white present?" he asked. "Peng, you're the closest, can you please give it to me?"

"If you insist," Peng answered.

Teddy unwrapped two smooth stones, both a warm dark gray color, like summer storm clouds. He saw immediately that each one had a thin white belt that went all the way around. "Lucky stones!" he cried. "These are lucky stones, aren't they? Did you give them to me, Peng?"

"I might have," said Peng.

"He did!" cried Prinny. "I saw him!"

"Thank you, Peng," said Teddy, because a bear can always use a little more luck, even if he has begun to think that he is already a very lucky bear indeed. He put them carefully down into his red wagon, close enough to touch whenever he wanted.

"I had to think of something," said Peng.

"You thought of a very good something," said Teddy, and then he couldn't wait any longer, not even to open the long box wrapped in paper that had polka dots of every color anyone has ever seen all over it. "Prinny, what is under the table?"

He thought Prinny would be the least able to keep anything a secret, and maybe he was right, but still, "I don't know," Prinny said. "Ask Umpah," she suggested. "Or Zia."

Before he had to ask, Umpah reached his trunk under the

table and pulled the shape out, while Zia kept a careful eye on it to be sure it stayed hidden under its pink sheet. Teddy stretched out from his wagon to pull on the sheet with both arms.

"I'll fold the sheet and put it away," Zia told him.

Teddy didn't even look at the sheet. He didn't look at Umpah, either. All of his attention was on the pile of tall sticks and coils of rope and heavy brown canvas. He was wondering what it was and guessing what it might be and hoping he had guessed correctly. He was hoping so hard that he didn't dare ask in words, so he just looked at Umpah.

Umpah nodded proudly.

"What is it?" Prinny wondered.

"A boat," Peng decided. "So Teddy and I can go around the island together."

"A hammock," Sid said, "so Teddy can sleep with me up in my beech when I sleep wrapped around a branch."

Teddy kept looking at Umpah, and hoping.

"Yes," Umpah said. "It is a tent. Zia sewed it, and I cut the sticks and found the rope. When it is a fine night, we will set it up, and you can sit in front of it and look at the stars until you are ready to go into it, and sleep."

"Oh," said Teddy. "Oh, Umpah, and oh, Zia, too—thank you, thank you."

"I wonder if a tent wouldn't be something a queen would like to have," Clara suggested, but Mr. B told her, "You could get dirty, sleeping outside, on the hard ground, in a tent."

"I could sleep in a tent," Sid offered. "I could sleep with you in your tent."

"Yes you could, sometimes, unless I wanted the adventure of sleeping alone," Teddy said.

"And could I sometimes too?" asked Prinny.

"Oh dear, oh dearie me, I don't know about that," Zia said.

"I could look after her," Teddy said. "Sid could help."

"And we could play with my present," Sid said. "Open mine, Teddy. I thought it up myself, and all the rules too, and once you've opened mine, we can eat the muffin cake while I explain."

Umpah passed out muffins from his cake, from the top first and then from the middle layer. There were enough muffins for everybody to have as many as they wanted, even Sid, and they were so tasty that Mr. B said, "Don't eat them all, Sid. I want to have a second one."

Sid swallowed three muffins and then took a rest, to explain the game of Explore, where you had to take turns listing what you could see going all the way around the island, and remember to start out with what every other player had said, and the list got longer and longer and harder and harder to remember, but if you forgot anything, everybody had to go back to the beginning and start over, but nobody was allowed to complain if that happened. "That's the most important rule," Sid told them as he reached out for his fourth muffin. "Because everybody can't remember everything all the time."

"That's a game that could last for a very long time, and maybe even never end," Peng warned.

"The perfect game for a rainy day!" Teddy cried. "Thank you, Sid. Games are the best presents," he said. Then, "Not the only best. Because hats and ruffs and lucky stones are also the best, and a tent, and a blueberry muffin cake, and chocolate ice cream too."

He thought for a minute. "This whole party is the best present," he decided.

"It was my idea!" cried Prinny, her four little feet dancing even faster. "I thought of it, didn't I, Zia? And I asked everybody, didn't I, everybody? And everybody wanted to do my idea!"

"Thank you, everybody," Teddy laughed. "And thank you, Prinny."

He looked down at the waves rushing up onto the sand. He looked over to the branches of the beech tree. He saw the stony hill where Peng had his cave and the two little houses, one pink, one red, and the pathway that led to the apple trees, where there was a white palace with a red door that he had had the idea for. He looked back at all of the guests at his party, and he felt glad and happy, lucky, and full of ideas for all of the new days lined up ahead, waiting to begin.

FPO
FINAL ART TK